Her Shadow

by

Sally Xerri-Brooks

First Edition November 2017

Copyright © 2017 Sally Xerri-Brooks

ISBN: 978-1973713876

Cover Design: Rosie Collin

Editor: Corinne Yaqub

Find out more at:

www.sallyxerribrooks.wordpress.com

Follow me on Twitter:

@salxerribrooks

Follow me on Instagram:

@mamabearsxb

Like me on Facebook:

www.facebook.com/sallyxerribrooks

All rights reserved.

This is a work of fiction. All characters and events in this publication are fictitious and any resemblance to real persons living or dead, places or events is purely coincidental.

Also by Sally Xerri-Brooks

Four Movements, available as an e-book.

For my wife Rachel – without whose encouragement, support and belief this book would never have been completed.

Also, for my daughter Gwyneth – without whom this book would have been finished many months earlier! Thank you for your inspiration.

Chapter one

"So it was £10,000 I said wasn't it?" She looked over her shoulder, seemingly oblivious to the open curtains that silhouetted her semi-naked figure against the window. I nodded from where I was sitting on the bed.

"Who should I make it payable to? I know cheques are a little passé, but the bank sends such beautiful ones these days, and it feels more authentic to sign my name in ink on this occasion. It means more." She scribbled away with a Mont Blanc fountain pen as she spoke, and I swiftly put my clothes back on. Sara was making no move towards gathering her Paul Smith suit, or shirt or bra, but I could feel the draught from the window, and the remaining paperwork waiting.

I reached for my satchel and grabbed the short form she needed to complete. I walked over and slid it along the edge of the desk to her, brushing her arm gently. I could see from the angle of her ears that she was smiling.

"I suppose you have others to see this morning?"

"I'm afraid so, Sara, although none will be in such beautiful surroundings." The mansion flat in Whitehall couldn't be her only residence, but the opulence of it, the original artwork that wouldn't be out of place in the Tate Modern and the clean lines of the furniture said a lot about the woman who spent time here.

Sara laughed. "Perhaps. When are you next passing through?"

"Next week," I said, and folded the proffered cheque, slipping it in my jacket pocket. I looked at my watch. I was late.

"You going to kiss me goodbye?" I smiled, bent, and gently kissed her. "Call me." She said.

At 8.30am when I had emerged at Marylebone there had been a chill, but the April sun was now beginning to warm Whitehall. I walked quickly towards the river and pulled out my mobile. "Hi Tom, it's Cam, can you call Sir Hugh's office and let them know I'm running late?"

"Did she give?" I could hear him rifling through papers on his desk as he spoke.

"Oh she really did."

"God, I can hear your smirk down the phone. I said you had a soft spot for her. Stop laughing at me and spill."

"Ten grand."

"Woo, good start to the day." There was a pause. "And?"

"Let's go for a drink later, sweetie."

"So mean! Ok, darling, give me a bell when you're on the train. I'll get in touch with Hughie."

I plunged back down into the underground and tried hard to wipe the smile off my face. I knew it made me look stupid and wouldn't play well with Sir Hugh. I emerged back into the sunshine and my phone bleeped.

//Meet Sir H at the restaurant, he'll meet you there. I mean it - I want the gossip! T x//

I turned on my heels and walked towards the bistro we often met at. I was welcomed at the door by a young male Eastern European waiter.

"I'm here to meet Sir Hugh." He nodded.

"He's at his usual table." He led me to a quiet corner, where Sir Hugh was pouring himself a generous glass of red wine.

"Ah, Miss Strawbank, how lovely to see you again." He stood to shake my hand and kissed my cheek, his bushy silver moustache and beard tickling my face. "Lovely perfume, my dear." I smiled. I usually don't wear perfume, so the only fragrance on me must have been the sophisticated scent that Sara was wearing earlier on. My face reddened.

"Sir Hugh, it's a pleasure as always." I sat down opposite him, and without asking he filled the huge wine glass that had appeared in front of me.

"Oh, just call me Hugh," he said, as always. He put his hand into the inside pocket of his silk lined tweed jacket and pulled out an envelope. "There you are my dear. Now we can just have a nice lunch and dispense with the ugly talk of money." I nodded my thanks and tucked the envelope into my own pocket, pretending that I wasn't keen to see how many noughts were on the end this time. I took a mouthful of wine, satisfied that this had already been a successful day for me professionally, and let it warm the back of my throat as it went down.

Sir Hugh thoroughly recommended the duck so we both tucked into the rich and refined dish delicately daubed in a plum jus. It worked well with the wine, clouding the edges of my thoughts slightly, which was no bad thing as Sir Hugh was regaling me with tales of his time at Knighton University College Medical School. My thoughts drifted back to this morning, and the way Sara had greeted me at the door, coffee mug in hand.

"There's still some in the pot - weapons grade strength or weak and feeble? You are Cameron Strawbank right? Fabulous name on a girl." I smiled at her.

"Weapons grade please," I said, "and I'm glad you like it. Most people expect me to be a guy. It's a tradition in my family for the oldest daughter to have a male name." I paused. "It could have been a lot worse - they could have called me Dave."

Sara Lorenzo MP threw her head back in laughter, her bracelets jangling. After handing me a cup of strong coffee she guided me to a room she described as her study. It was twice the size of my apartment.

"Well Cameron, I think we're going to get on well. Take a seat and tell me about Knighton and how things are going there."

Sir Hugh placed his hand on my wrist, bringing me back to his macabre story. "So I said to Nobby, it's one thing scaring a fellow medic with an unexpected body part, but startling a poor young English undergraduate with a cadaver's finger in her lunch box is just not de rigueur." I nodded, trying to hide my disgust, and taking another sip of my wine to overcome the queasiness I felt.

"Of course he's one of the nation's foremost minds on heart disease these days. But then I suppose medicine attracts that sort." I was wondering what sort that was when Sir Hugh spoke again. "But now then, here's me going on about me and my old college days. You weren't even born then! Heavens. So dear, are you courting?"

"Not at the moment," I said.

"Ah well, the right fellow will come along my dear. They just get a bit scared off by your type."

"My type?"

"Well, you know, brainy, trouser-wearing, that kind of thing." I smiled uncertainly, deciding that feminism may have passed Sir Hugh by. His cheque was warm in my pocket, and I was still basking in the glow of the morning too much to make any kind of witty comeback. "Anyway, I like you, Miss Strawbank. I think you're splendid."

I wonder what he would have thought if he knew about what had happened with the MP for Mallington South.

The coffee Sara made was good, strong and smooth, with a hint of chocolate. It was as decadent as my surroundings, and I felt at ease. My meetings were variously formal, informal, convivial and awkward. If I was lucky they were friendly - as this one was starting to be. My job was to work out which version of Cameron to be - formal, relaxed, witty, quiet or outspoken. The better the meeting, the better the outcome.

"Are you here to ask me for money?" She asked quickly.

"Well, I won't deny that the subject will come up. But first, I want to find out more about you, what you care about, what you think about Knighton, and how we might work together."

"You and me?"

"Well, us and the college." Sara sipped her coffee.

"I see. Well here you go, I studied biochemistry and hated every minute of it. I should have studied English or Politics or some such, but I was under the misguided impression it would satisfy my mother's desire for me to be a success."

"I, er, so you didn't enjoy your time at Knighton then?" I fingered my coffee mug.

"Oh I loved it. In spite of the course you see. I did everything, played tennis in the summer, hockey in the winter, took part in the debating society and set up a women's group. It was all about freedom for me. It wasn't the degree, it was the experience."

I relaxed again, and started to work through possible projects in my mind. I crossed off academic scholarships and scientific research straight away, and stared to think more creatively.

"I just feel I was so lucky." I nodded, urging her to continue. It was critical that she was allowed to just talk at this point. "I got a grant and was able to live on it without working in some dingy bar every night. My parents weren't poor, but they weren't rich either, and I was able to be financially independent." A light went on in my head.

"Yes, things have changed so much, even since I was studying."

"That can't have been so long ago surely. How old are you?" It was one of the less personal questions I had been asked in the course of this job, so I just answered her.

"32. Old enough to have seen a change." Sara smiled as if weighing something up. "Sadly, we know that lots of youngsters now decide against higher education because of the fear of debt, It's just so tragic." Sara poured herself some more coffee and topped mine up without asking if I wanted more. I smiled my thanks and wondered what the caffeine would do to me - I always drank too much coffee on my London days.

"Well, we've decided we can do better," I said, leaning forward in my seat, "and we've established grants for those from low income families who are on course for good results at A level." Sara's eyes lit up, and she caught the hand with which I had been gesticulating.

"Brilliant. You know, I voted against the top-up fees." I nodded. I did know, it had been in the research file Tom had prepared for me that I had read on the train. She shook her head. "It breaks my heart to think of those poor kids in school desperate to get on." She dropped my hand and looked up, making eye contact. "What did you study?"

I smiled, ready for the inevitable put down as I said "Media Studies". But Sara remained serious.

"At Knighton?"

"No, I never would have got in. I studied in Yorkshire."

"You're too modest Cameron. I think you've got it all worked out." I raised my eyebrows, not completely sure what she meant. "Will ten do?"

"Sorry?"

"Ten thousand pounds? That will help five students right?" This was big for a first gift and I was taken aback. I worked to keep my cool.

"Well six actually if you include Gift Aid. I must say, that's very generous of you." Sara took a sip from her coffee cup, smiling ruefully.

"Maybe it is generosity. But sometimes I wonder it isn't to assuage my own guilt." She gestured to the room around her.

"Success isn't a bad thing," I said quietly, surprised at her candour.

"At the cost of what though? And you, you seem like you know the work well. Do students get a lot out of it?"

I smiled broadly at this. I had met many of the bursary students and in almost every case I'd been impressed by them and what they had managed to achieve. I told her about it, describing a couple of students' personal experiences.

Sara nodded. "You know this is a good investment, Cameron. And if you are satisfied, then so am I." I smiled uncertainly. She was looking directly at me, not quite smiling. I broke eye contact, beginning to feel exposed, but not sure why.

"I like to think I know the projects well. It's my job to."

"Indeed," said Sara with a knowing smile. I blushed slightly and looked at my hands, which were still fiddling with my now empty mug. I willed them to stop. Sara reached over, and I held my breath as her hand approached mine. Her fingertips grazed my knuckles as she took my cup, and her own, and put them on the coffee table. "I like your style Cameron."

"Er thank you," I blushed again, beginning to feel like a teenager. "You can call me Cam you know. All my friends do."

"Am I a friend now?" Sara laughed. "I'm sorry, Cam, I'm teasing. You are just such a refreshing change from all the dull meetings I have every day." She paused. "And you have the most extraordinary eyes."

Startled, I looked directly at her. She smiled and touched her lips to mine. I sprang back.

"Sorry, I didn't mean to surprise you. Am I getting the vibes that you have a girlfriend?"

"No, I..."

"Me neither. And I don't want you to feel uncomfortable. So if you'd rather we pretended that never happened, I can go through to the kitchen and get more coffee."

"I don't think I can take any more coffee." I leaned forward and kissed the MP for Mallington South back, sweeping ethical concerns to the back of my caffeine-drenched mind. I wasn't sure if it was the coffee jitters, but I felt pins and needles begin in my hands, which had found their way to her waist.

"No," she said, pulling away slightly, "I don't think coffee is what we need right now."

Sir Hugh drained his glass, his cheeks glowing from the rich lunch. "Well, Miss Strawbank, I will let you go about your business." I proffered my credit card. He shook his head. "Oh no, no, no my dear, I insist." I knew better than to argue. I offered my hand to shake his. He took it weakly and leaned in to give me another damp kiss on the cheek.

I read the cheque on the tube back to the station. £1,500. All in all, it hadn't been a bad day's work.

Chapter 2

There was a gin and tonic on the bar waiting for me, beside a grinning Tom. His perfectly styled hair and beautifully fitting grey suit with purple lining made his slim figure stand out. We often met here at the end of the day. He lived in the city centre, so stopping for a drink near his swanky flat had become a habit at the end of a London day.

"You wouldn't believe what Damien's on now," he said, "I mean really, the man's a nightmare." He rolled his eyes and sipped his prosecco at the same time. A well-honed skill.

"Target tantrum, or team building bonding session?" I asked, having a generous slurp of my drink.

"Somewhere between the two. Honestly, it's as though he's swallowed every management success book written, and speaks solely in some garbled blue sky deep dive hybrid language." I laughed. It was true, Damien was our head of department, and while he was mostly a nice bloke, he lapsed into corporate madness from time to time.

"Anyway, enough about him. Tell me about your day." Tom turned his bright green eyes on me, and I felt myself go bright red. He laughed. "Come on!"

"Ok, but I need another of these first. A double." Tom signalled to the barman who began preparing another G and T. I drained my glass and replaced it with the new one.

"So, I finally met Sara Lorenzo."

"What was her apartment like? I saw how much it sold for when I did the research. I bet she's got gorgeous taste."

"Oh yes," I said, "it really is beautiful. And you know, she's pretty cool too."

"I knew you had a crush. What does she look like in the flesh? Is she all wrinkly and old up close?"

"No, she's beautiful," I said, trying and failing to add an ironic tone to my voice, trying not to sound as sappy as I felt. "In fact, she, um, we..." I tailed off. Tom said nothing, waiting for the inevitable sharing. He knew I was too far into this story to back out. He raised his eyebrows slowly.

"You didn't?" I peered at him from under my eye lashes. "Oh my God, you did!" I laughed, relieved to be able to tell my story. "Ok, I want every single little gory detail!"

I took another slurp of gin and tonic and told him the story. He was on his third glass of prosecco by the time I finished. "So did she give you the cheque before or after?" I gave him a shove.

"She agreed to the donation within about ten minutes of me arriving."

"But she paid you after right?"

"I can't imagine what you mean." I fiddled with the serviette my glass was sitting on and for the first time that day felt discomfort about what had happened.

"Hmmm. So, will you see her again?"

"Well, she joked I should drop in next time I'm in town."

"She's smitten." I laughed and shook my head. It was unlikely. She presumably had her pick. Even so, later on that evening I couldn't help but watch the political news on the TV more intently in case I caught a glimpse of the Shadow Health Secretary – Sara Lorenzo.

The following week I found myself in the wilds of Yorkshire, visiting a medical graduate from the college. Dr Catherine Smart lived in what could only be described as a fairy-tale cottage. The front door was down a winding path overgrown with lavender and roses. The resulting fragrance was overwhelming but not unpleasant. While the door was not hewn from gingerbread, it did house a stern sticker warning that the occupier did not buy from the door. I pressed the doorbell that looked generations old, wondering if it still worked. I heard what sounded like a gong clang from the depths beyond the door. For at least a minute there was no sound. It wouldn't be the first time an appointment had been abandoned without warning. Finally though, I heard a heavy lock turn and the wooden door slowly opened.

"Dr Smart?" Her 80-year-old face was lined and her mouth was in a straight line, but when she glanced at the pin badge on my lapel that carried the crest of the college, she smiled warmly.

"I've just put the kettle on, do come in."

I was shown into a cosy living room that looked like it had last been decorated in the 1960s. It was tidy and well cared for, and I spotted a laptop sitting on an old bureau. Dr Smart treated me to a dainty cup of Earl Grey in a bone china cup and saucer decorated in a geometric design. I asked the same question I asked all the others. "How was your time at the college?"

"Jolly hard work. Many of the lecturers were very suspicious of me and Gladys Murphy. We were the only girls studying medicine, and while we weren't the first, there were many who felt we were taking the place of a more deserving man. So we had the challenge of the subject, and so much more to prove than the chaps. There were some real duds too, but somehow they got through on a nod and a wink from one or other of the profs."

"It's a stark comparison to now," I said. "There are more girls studying medicine now than boys at the college." Dr Smart smiled, and sighed.

"Things change." she said. She began telling me which of the halls of residence she lived in, and tales of getting caught out after lights out. I looked around the room. I searched for the usual clues - family photographs, books, paintings - anything that would tell me more about the person, something to spark a conversation. I noticed a small black and white wedding photo in a simple frame on the bureau.

"Is this you?" I asked. She looked at the picture and smiled at the young man and woman smiling, wearing modest wedding attire.

"Yes. Gerald was on the course too, dear chap. He wasn't one of the duds of course!" I laughed. She touched her wedding ring as she went on. "He was an accomplished neurosurgeon in the end. Life wasn't always easy for him. He saved and changed countless lives though he never saw that. Died in 1987."

"You must miss him."

"Well yes, I suppose so. But you know, while my life changed after he was gone, and I found it very hard to start with, I found a way to be. There are things I do now that I would never have done with him. He hated travelling, and since 1991 I've visited every continent. I'm happy. I think of him fondly, and sometimes feel the pull of the past, but I wonder if I genuinely miss him now?" I let the question hang. She wasn't really asking me.

"What was your specialism?"

"Well, I started as a general surgeon in the hospital Gerald worked at. But I ended up as a breast cancer specialist." She took a sip from her tea. "The men didn't want to do breasts. I was the only woman, so it ended up as my job."

I wasn't sure what to say. She wasn't saying it to shock me, she was just telling me the facts of her career.

"Of course things changed a great deal over the years. We learnt a lot more about the disease, how best to treat it, when to operate and how far to go. I still keep up to date with the journals," she said, gesturing to the sleek computer I had noticed earlier, "and the advances being made in identifying the genes that cause some kinds of breast cancer are really impressive."

"Yes, I had the pleasure of visiting the lab where some of the college research takes place. There's a really great team of academics using cell lines to learn more about some of those genes." Dr Smart raised her eyebrows, as though she hadn't expected me to know as much as I had just shared with her. I felt mildly smug as I took a modest sip of my tea. "I could arrange for you to have a look around the lab and meet some of the researchers if it is of interest?"

"That sounds like a great idea. I'd love to. I'll get my diary." She wasn't gone long, and had put some smart reading glasses on as she flicked through the pages. "Now, I am away for a while doing a tour of South America. However, perhaps after that?"

"Sounds good, I'll speak to the research team and get a few suggested dates from them and get back to you. Do you use email?"

"Yes, it's the most efficient way. Pass your notepad over, I'll scribble my address down." It wasn't long after that that she made it clear that our meeting was concluded. We hadn't talked about donations or anything of that kind, but I got the sense that she knew why I was there. I would be seeing her again in a few weeks and I already knew she would be hooked by the scenes in the lab. I made a mental note to make sure that I set the visit up within the next 24 hours. I felt that Dr Smart would appreciate efficiency.

The drive home was long and dull. After a couple of hours I stopped for coffee at a service station. I sat down for a flat white and pulled my phone out of my pocket. There was a message from Sara. I hadn't heard from her since I left her apartment and hadn't made any effort to contact her. It had been one of those moments, almost perfect in its composition, and somehow I didn't want to ruin it by adding reality to it. Added to this, I had no idea how often she did that kind of thing. Surely she could take her pick, so I doubted I was anything more than a momentary piece of fluff. I didn't mind that, but didn't want to start hoping for something I knew wouldn't happen. Nonetheless, the appearance of her name on the screen of my phone sent a bubble of excitement up my spine.

//So you're trying to play it cool are you Strawbank? Figures ;) When are you next in London? X //

I immediately began to analyse the text. One kiss – did that signify that she liked me, or was it something she put on the end of all texts? What did the wink after 'figures' mean? Had she read something into my actions that I hadn't intended? She wanted to know when I was next in London though, that was a good thing right?

I looked at the diary on my phone. I was due in London the following week for some meetings. I started writing a reply, and then stopped. I couldn't reply immediately, it would make me look desperate, as though I had been sitting on the floor of my kitchen, hugging a bar of Galaxy, looking at my phone with longing eyes, waiting for a text from Sara after what was almost certainly just a one-time thing. I looked at my watch. I would have my coffee, read the paper, and then text her.

I opened the paper and began to read the headlines. It didn't take me long to give that up though. I spent the next 20 minutes drafting the perfect off-hand response that would have the correct tone and look as though I had barely thought about it. This was tough stuff. I went and got some sugar for my coffee. The drive and the mental effort needed rewarding with something sweet.

Eventually I settled for a simple message that wouldn't give much away.

//Ha ha! No, not playing it cool, just travelling a lot. I'm in London next Thursday if you're about at all. x//

I sent it and then immediately read it back. My palms were sweaty. It was too matey, no flirting, nothing. So much for the planning of the message. She would think I was a total pleb and not interested at all. I turned the phone onto silent and stuffed it back into my pocket. I didn't want to see the response – or lack thereof. I sighed, ran my hand through my hair, and made my way back to the car. It was time to head home.

I pulled into the underground car park of the development I lived in an hour later. I turned off the engine and closed my eyes for a few seconds. I was tired. It had been a long day; Lots of driving, lots of caffeine, and not enough real food. I got out of the car and made my way to the lift that would take me up to my fourth floor apartment. It wasn't until I had walked into the kitchen, switched on the kettle, and opened the fridge that I remembered I hadn't done any shopping. I rolled my eyes. I had no one to blame but myself. I had meant to drop into a supermarket on my way home. How had one little text message thrown me so much? I took my phone out of my pocket, hardly wanting to look for fear of the inevitable blank screen. I took a deep breath and peeped at the display. Two messages. One from Tom.

//Fancy a curry and a pint Cam? My cupboards are bare and I need a drink! X // I smiled.

The second was from Sara. I felt the excitement rise in my stomach again, and mentally berated myself for behaving like a teenager.

//Thursday's perfect. I want to take you to lunch – 1pm at the Oracle. See you there. Xx//

I selected the number and called. "Hi, it's me, yup, that sounds great. No, I'm fine. Yeah, just a good day that's all. What do you mean? I'm always chipper aren't I?? Ok, see you at the Sultan in 10." I cancelled the call to Tom, smiled to myself, and then checked the time that Sara's text had arrived – three minutes after I had sent my message. She clearly had no fears about appearing too eager. And yet somehow she still seemed cool and unruffled. I needed to learn that. I quickly wrote a message, dumped my work bag, and locked up the flat.

//It's a date xx//

Chapter 3

Tom and I ate at the curry house that was equidistant from our two places so regularly that the staff there knew us by name. We almost always ordered the same thing and sat at the same table, so it was kind of like an extension of our respective living rooms really.

The poppadums arrived alongside an Indian beer for each of us within seconds of arriving, and soon we were tucking in and catching up about our days.

"What was your old dear like?" asked Tom.

"She wasn't really like an old dear. I hope I'm like her when I'm her age." I told him about the meeting.

"Sounds like she might be good for a legacy," he said.

"God, you're so mercenary!"

"Perhaps you need to be more mercenary. You know the rules, you're not allowed to leave until you've asked for a grand on your first visit."

"The rules according to Damien. Bugger him, I'm on track to meet my target and I've never followed his wretched rules." Tom laughed.

"Are you back in the office tomorrow?"

"Yes, heaps of paperwork. I need to organise a lab visit for Dr Smart as well. I've got a researcher who I think would love to meet her," I said.

"Female I suppose."

"And?"

"Just saying you're on a bit of a roll at the moment…" Our main courses arrived and Tom started to tear into the naan bread.

"Oh behave. It stands to reason that one of the first wave of female surgeons would appreciate meeting a woman. Anyway, Sara doesn't count as a roll." I scraped half the rice onto my plate and helped myself to a generous portion of tikka masala.

"You're so seeing her again aren't you?" I said nothing, knowing he could see it in my eyes. "When?"

"Not telling."

"You know what Cam, it's about time you met someone. Not sure if Sara will be your happily ever after, but I'm glad you're having fun. You know, after…" he took a mouthful of his bhuna. I stuck my tongue out at him and asked him about his plans for the weekend.

The next day I spent several hours looking at research Tom had put together on prospects – potential donors. There was something wistful about the name, as though we were using little sieves in the Wild West to hunt for gold. There were some parallels, but this was altogether a more political experience. My list consisted of 76 individuals, each of whom had shared information publicly that indicated to Tom that they might be in a position to give a four, five or six figure gift. This might be through being named in a publicly available annual report as being on a high salary, or because their postcode put them in an expensive area, or because they were on a local or national rich list. There were other ways too, but those were the main ones. They all had one thing in common – they had all studied at Knighton University College. My job was to piece that information together and create a real relationship with each of those individuals that was based on them as a person. Regardless of what was written in one of Tom's excellent and very detailed reports, nothing was a given. It simply gave you a better run up.

I picked up the phone. I needed to set up some more meetings. More meetings meant more opportunities to ask for a contribution. More asks meant more people saying yes. It was a numbers game. The first four calls I made to prospects went through to personal assistants who all said they would get back to me. This was often a polite way of saying "no." I made a note in my diary to follow them up next week if I hadn't heard from them by then. The fifth call was more promising.

"Hi, is that Mr Lockwood?"

"Yes. Who is this?"

"Cameron Strawbank, from Knighton University College. I wanted to make contact with you. I'm in London next week meeting up with high profile alumni like yourself, and wondered if you'd be available for a coffee and a chat perhaps?" I knew his office was based there, and an existing visit was a great context for an invitation. Somehow people seemed to feel less under pressure and more likely to say yes if they knew you were in the area anyway.

"Well, I don't know if I can be any use to you – what do you want to talk about?" He sounded hesitant, but he hadn't said no straight away. This was going well.

"It would be great to hear about your time at the college, and share some of our news with you in person. I'd also love to get your feedback on some of our new projects. There might even be an opportunity for you to help in some way." There was a pause.

"Ok, well, I have about half an hour to spare on Thursday morning." I silently clenched my fist and made the arrangement with him.

Chapter 4

Sunlight poured through the gap between the curtains of my bedroom. Drifting in and out of sleep knowing it was late in the morning and I had no commitments felt luxurious. I yawned and star-fished across the bed. Having a double bed all to myself didn't always feel like a treat, but this morning I owned it completely and enjoyed the space. I rolled over and grabbed my phone. It was almost 11am. I smiled and ruffled my hair. I could see dust particles dancing in the shafts of light. There was an unopened message on the screen with Sara's name attached. I put the phone back down and hugged myself. Delayed gratification.

I got up and stepped into the shower. Once I was out and wrapped in my towel I allowed myself to return to the phone.

//Morning. I hope you're having a more relaxing time than me. Constituency surgery :/ Looking forward to Thurs xx //

I dressed and walked out of the flat. The leaves on the trees that lined the road were a brilliant bright green. The smell of car exhausts and freshly cut grass filled my nostrils. I unzipped my jacket. It was time for brunch – an occasional treat I allowed myself at a café nearby.

I ordered coffee, orange juice, a vegetarian cooked breakfast and extra toast. I was starving and it felt like it had been days since I'd last eaten. I laid out the café's newspaper in front of me, and lost myself in current affairs of countries miles from me.

I was on my second coffee, contemplating the text back to Sara when I heard a familiar voice. "Hi." I looked up and immediately put down my coffee and stood up.

"Hi, I wasn't expecting to see you here." It was a stupid thing to say and I felt every stupid word like a thick book falling down a flight of steps. Of course I wasn't expecting Hayley. And of course she knew that. My cheeks were hot. I was unsure whether I should hug her or not. The decision was taken out of my hands. Hayley swept back her blond locks and gave me a peck on the cheek.

"Mind if I join you?" She asked.

"Of course." She smiled and turned to make her order at the counter. I couldn't believe I had put myself in this position. Why on earth had I agreed? Why hadn't I told her I was about to leave? It was too late now.

I looked at her profile as she chatted to the guy behind the counter. I remembered the first time I met her, a year and a half ago. Our eyes had met over drunken friends in the toilets in a nightclub in town. I wasn't much of a clubber, and holding the hair of a friend behind her head as she spewed up the meal we'd shared earlier wasn't my idea of fun.

As I tidied up my friend, wiping her mouth and making vaguely comforting sounds, the woman I had just shared a sympathetic look with spoke. "I vote we put these two in cabs home and then go and get some tequila." She was helping her friend find her other stiletto which seemed to have disappeared. I laughed, and ushered my friend out of the toilets. I didn't expect to see her again.

I eventually did put my friend in a cab. I was standing at the rank waiting for another to arrive to take me home, when I heard her voice again. "What happened to the tequila?" We didn't drink tequila in the end. We found a bar that was still serving and ordered coffee.

I made a show of reading a long article about the Middle East when she came back over with a pink milkshake. She sat down. I looked up. "What, no coffee?"

She laughed. "Not this time, Cam. How are you doing?"

"Well, thanks. Work's busy, in a good way."

"Still flirting for money then?" I smiled at the joke she had made so many times before, feeling a warmth inside that I had hoped was dormant.

"Yes thanks."

"How's your target looking this year?"

"£800k." Hayley raised her eyebrows.

"They get a lot for their money with you, don't they? That's some return on investment. I hope you've been given a pay rise recently." I laughed, we both knew that was unlikely. She was sitting opposite me, and I could smell her hair. Freshly washed, it took me back to that first night. We had ended up at her house, talking all night. I remember that by about 4am I was beginning to feel so sleep deprived that my mind was wandering into strange places.

I was lying on a sofa in Hayley's living room. She had just gone to the kitchen to get herself a glass of water, and I was beginning to doze off. It was midsummer, and the sun was already beginning to rise. My mind was drifting, and I stirred slightly, surprised to find myself somewhere other than my own bed. I dropped off again, and was awoken just a few moments later by Hayley's lips softy kissing mine. There was something familiar, soothing, and also exciting about it.

"Come on sleepyhead. We've talked enough. Bed time." She took my hand and led me to her bedroom, which smelled of freshly laundered linen. I laid down, burying my head in a deep soft pillow, and fell immediately into a deep sleep.

"So, what's the news with you?" I asked. Hayley looked down at her drink before answering.

"Oh, you know, the usual."

"Not really, you've got to give me more than that." She gave me a wry smile.

"Ok, work is pretty much the same, although I have been promoted."

"Again? Good for you. And your love life?"

"Oh, you know. There's someone, but nothing serious." I resisted the temptation to roll my eyes. It was ever thus with Hayley. I also resisted the temptation to press for more. But that would suggest I was interested.

"Keeping yourself busy then," I said.

"It's been too long Cam, I've missed you." She looked directly at me. I couldn't help but look away.

I had woken later on that morning, for a moment confused as to where I was. I opened my eyes to see Hayley looking at me. Her face was inscrutable, but the minute I remembered where I was, and our night of endless conversation I smiled. So did she. Then she kissed me, and I inhaled her sleepy laundry scent. Having regained some energy this time it didn't stop at a kiss. We were warm and safe in a beautiful pale yellow bedroom in luxurious linen, far away from the rest of the world. The sex was gentle, slow and hot. It was a couple of hours later that she ventured out of bed to prepare the cafetiere that filled her room with a delicious aroma. My skin was still tingling as I sipped the strong tasting liquid. I could hear the radio gently playing quietly in the kitchen.

"Here's to drunken friends," I said.

"Yeah, definitely. Here's to you too. You look beautiful when you're asleep you know. I watched you." I raised my eyebrows. "Not in a stalker way. Heavens, you're in my bed, I'm allowed to look at you."

"Can I buy you breakfast?" I asked. She agreed, and so I had taken her to the café where we both sat now.

"You've missed me?" I paused, gathering my thoughts. "You've not been in touch though."

"I didn't think you wanted to hear from me."

"Perhaps at first. But I missed you too."

"Missed? But you're over it now?" she said. I frowned. "Sorry, unfair of me to ask."

"Well, it's been a year or something," I said. It had been 11 and a half months almost to the day.

I wanted to tell her that I was urging her to draw out her milkshake for as long as possible so we could talk more – something we had always done with such ease. We fell into comfortable conversation, talking about work, and mutual friends.

"And how about you Cam? Anyone special for you?"

"Well, not sure really." I fingered the sugar bowl which was filled with artistically shaped sugar lumps – purposely designed to look natural and rough around the edges I supposed. She smiled.

"So there is someone! Come on, who is she?"

"Too early to say. We've only met once."

"She's obviously made an impression."

"We'll see. More milkshake?"

"No thanks, I've got to dash. Meeting a friend." I cursed myself for the disappointment I felt.

"Yes, I guess I should get off too really." After a few more minutes of small talk, Hayley pulled on her jacket. She stood up and smiled.

"We should do this more often," she said. I nodded, knowing it would be foolhardy to take her up on her offer. I gathered my possessions and stood up too. She leaned forward and pulled me into a hug, departing with a kiss on my cheek. I breathed a long, slow breath out as she walked away. My insides felt as though they had been lightly whisked.

I walked back towards my apartment, remembering the night 11 and a half months ago. We'd had dinner at a local restaurant, and shared a bottle of wine. We were walking along this very road, arm in arm. "You know how I feel about you, Hayley," I said, bumping my shoulder up against hers.

"Darling, it's been five months, and we've barely spent a weekend apart. I know how you feel. So, your place or mine?"

"No, I mean it. I really think that…" But I didn't have a chance to finish.

"Hey, cocktails, look," she pointed at a neon sign. "I fancy a mojito. Let's go in!" I followed in her wake. She ordered two, and perched at a stool by the bar, ushering me to sit beside her. The bar was busy, and there were people either side of us.

"So this is a bit convenient isn't it?"

"Sorry babe? What?" She waved her debit card at the barman.

"Surrounded by people, loud music, plenty of booze."

"All good so far. But I think you're trying to say something different. Am I right?"

"Yes," I said, hoping to sound less like the sullen teenager I knew I was channelling.

"Come on, Cam, drink up, this'll cheer you up."

"No," I raised my voice both to be heard over the noise and because a fizzing bubble of anger had reached my mouth unexpectedly. "No, not this time." Hayley raised her eyebrows and looked at me, saying nothing for a moment. I didn't know where to go next, what to say, so I stood up, grabbed my coat, and walked out of the bar. I started walking with purpose back towards my flat.

Within a few seconds, I heard footsteps behind me. I concentrated on not turning around. Hayley's voice sounded calm. "Cameron, for God's sake, turn around." I said nothing and carried on walking. "Cam. Please." I slowed. "What have I done?" A few more steps. I stopped and turned to face her.

"Every time I try and talk to you about anything that matters, any time I want to be serious, you fob me off." She opened her mouth but I waved my hand. "No, not this time, you're not going to make a silly joke, or drag me into another bar, or kiss me to shut me up. You are so infuriating. I barely know whether I hate you or love you." I stopped. Hayley wasn't trying to talk anymore. "You see, and all the times I've tried to tell you that, that I love you, that I want more than just dinner and sex every week, and you know that, don't you?"

"Yes." She took my arm, and I let her. We carried on walking, this time in silence. Once in my flat, she put on the kettle and made me a cup of tea. "Yes, you're right. I know, I've known for a while. I'm sorry, I'm emotionally stunted, I'm an arse, I like cocktails and dinner and sex and fun and I don't like talking about feelings. Ok, yes."

We were sitting in the lounge. "Well, I can't do it anymore. I love you, and I don't care if it makes you feel awkward. I can't pretend that this is just some fling that doesn't mean anything. It means something. We're worth something."

"You're right. You do mean something. You're worth more than I ever tell you," she said handing me my mug of tea.

"So can we just talk about this, where we're going, what we're doing?" I could feel tears gathering in my eyes and blinked a few times to try and delay them falling.

"I just know that I can only disappoint you. I don't want to settle down, I don't want to be someone's partner, I don't want to be your wife."

"I'm not proposing you idiot. I just want to explore the possibilities."

"I'm not sure there are any beyond this."

"So that's it?" I struggled to keep my voice level, knowing if I said any more I would cry.

"Don't misunderstand me. It's not that I don't care about you, Cam, it's just that I can't do any more than this for now."

"For how long?" I knew I was losing my composure, but I wasn't sure it mattered.

"I don't know." I clasped my hands together.

"I can't live on a knife edge, Hayley. It's too unbalanced, and the more this goes on, the more unbalanced it will get."

She frowned, and then put her arms around me. We stayed there, motionless, in each other's arms. After what felt like several minutes, but was probably only a few seconds, I began to feel her teardrops on my shoulder. She pulled away.

"You're right, Cam. You need more. I can't give it." I didn't know what to say. "I'll go."

And that had been it.

There had been a couple of awkward meetings to exchange things, or just accidentally running into each other, but no real conversation since that night. After she had gone I replayed the conversation in my head angrily, trying to think of a better way of expressing myself. Not that I could change things now. In my more maudlin moments I berated myself for pushing too hard. What would have happened if I'd said nothing?

Chapter 5

Thursday morning came and I found myself in the offices of a large insurance company. I walked to the reception desk, where a woman in a headset took my name. "I'm here to see Mr Lockwood." She printed me an ID badge, and then took me down a corridor and showed me to a meeting room constructed almost entirely of glass, bar one wall, which was a dark polished wood. From the window, which took up one side of the cube I was in, I could see across central London. I was on the ninth floor, so there was quite a view. There was a cafetiere on a side table, so I poured myself a coffee and sat in an expensive leather seat at the board room style table.

By the time my prospect arrived I had almost finished my coffee. I stood up to shake his hand. Despite his 43 years, Martin Lockwood looked youthful. My research pack told me he was Director of European Markets, although in reality I had very little grasp of what that meant. Slim, with short blond hair, he gave me a brusque smile before offering me more coffee and pouring one for himself.

"So, what's all this about?" He was clearly not a man given to small talk.

"Well, things are changing at Knighton. We're evolving and looking to the future, but we need people like you to be part of that change." I paused, gauging his response. He said nothing, so I continued. His face was blank. "We want to provide our students and researchers with the business experience and acumen that can make them as successful as people like you." There was a flicker of recognition on his face.

"Go on."

"And in order to do that we need role models. For each aspiring student who has the ability, we want to provide a business mentor to guide them through their entrepreneurial development."

"God, I never had any of that. I just had to make my own way," he said, looking at his mobile. "What I really want to know is, where are the really decent graduates? Frankly, the ones we've had from Knighton recently have been crap. No get up and go, no initiative. When I was their age I'd already been working for three years, funding my own degree. These kids haven't a clue about what it takes."

I nodded. He was in full flow, and I didn't want to interrupt him before he'd made the point he was working up to.

"I didn't need a mentor, I just needed a shot, and I was lucky enough to get one. Yes, of course, luck counts for a lot, but it's all about hard work and just getting on with it. I couldn't care less about these youngsters' gap years or work experience. What matters is a bit of determination."

He was beginning to sound like a caricature of Alan Sugar, which gave me an idea.

"So, for you it's about these youngsters doing it for themselves?"

"Exactly." He folded his arms and gave me a hard stare.

"You may be interested in our final year business students." No response from across the table. "They undertake a year-long project, establishing businesses from scratch. They can carry out any activity they wish, and all they are given is £1,000 start-up funds. What they do beyond that is up to them. Critically, the investor gets a proportion of profits." He raised his eyebrows. "So one of my tasks is to find people who are willing to not only invest in these businesses, but become partners."

He sucked in his cheeks and looked up to the top left corner of the cube. "Like an angel investor?"

Bingo. I had him. "Yes, exactly that." I knew it was important to not say too much here.

"And the investors get to choose which businesses they invest in?" He unfolded his arms.

"Yes." He took a sip from his coffee and then paused for a moment. I smiled but kept my mouth shut.

"Ok. I'll come in and see these kids, but on the condition I part with no money unless I see a business idea that is good enough."

"Sounds perfect." I smiled. The next round was coming up in four months, so I'd need to keep him warm until then. "In the meantime though, we're inviting some of our more influential alumni to the House of Lords for a drinks reception in a few weeks' time. It would be my pleasure to invite you there."

"Check with my p.a. on your way out. If I'm free, I'll come." He was already standing up. The meeting was over.

Lunch with Sara was a stylish affair. I met her in a small bistro in Bloomsbury where she had already ordered two glasses of prosecco. Not accustomed to bubbles so early in the day, the first sip made me giggle. "Crikey, anyone would think you were a cheap date, Cam," said Sara.

"Oh I am I'm afraid. Sorry to disappoint." I gave a cheeky smile and took another sip. We lunched on risotto and talked about our day so far. It felt like a first date. I wasn't sure what it really was. It had crossed my mind it might simply be a high class booty call. I asked her about her work, it seemed a safe bet.

"It's all about the next General Election for us I'm afraid. I'm spending more time than usual in my constituency campaigning, as well as doing my usual local duties, and in Westminster it's all strategy meetings and whispering in corners. We still don't know the date of course, but it will be some time in the next 18 months."

"Will you win this time?" I asked, genuinely interested, having been a keen follower of politics. In fact, that was why Tom had given me Sara to meet in the first place.

"Do you want the party line or the official answer?" smiled Sara, peering over her third glass of fizz. I laughed. "Honestly, I don't know. He's a good leader, but you and I both know the media haven't really taken to him, and in this day and age, that's a big deal."

"He always comes over as thoroughly decent to me. Perhaps a little goofy." Sara laughed.

"I'll tell him you said that, I'm having dinner with him and his wife tomorrow night." I blushed.

"Oh god, I'm sorry, I didn't mean to offend you. He's just a bloke on the telly to me; it's easy to forget he's a real live person."

"Oh don't worry," said Sara, briefly resting her hand on my own, "he's had far worse. I'm not offended. Besides, you look cute when you're embarrassed."

When the bill came I reached for it, but Sara got there first. "No Cameron, this is my treat." Her look courted no contradiction, so I thanked her and began to gather my possessions together. "Shall we go back to my place and check the coffee machine still works?"

"I thought you'd never ask." My stomach turned over, and I counted myself lucky that I had no further meetings that afternoon. I wondered where Sara was supposed to be. Somewhere in the corridors of power probably.

I had watched her mouth throughout lunch, eating, drinking, talking, laughing and longed to kiss it. The prosecco had dulled my inhibition, so as we walked through her front door I tugged off her jacket and brought my lips to hers as I shrugged my coat off. I could feel her smiling, as she pulled away, took my hand and led me to her bedroom. She laid me back on her bed, removed her top and laid on top of me, kissing me and allowing her hands to roam down my body. She tasted of prosecco and smelled lightly of fine perfume. Her touch made me tingle and I struggled to keep my composure. She pulled at my top and then my bra, and it wasn't long before we were both naked.

"Where are my manners?" She murmured after a while. "I haven't even made you that coffee yet." I groaned and pulled her closer.

"Fuck the coffee," I said.

"The coffee? Are you sure?"

"You are pure filth, Sara, you know that right?"

"You think so?" She teased, as she kissed my breasts and made me long for her to take her hand lower. And then she did.

An hour later we were lazing end to end in the opulent bath, which was filled with gorgeously scented oils. "I've got to go soon, darling," said Sara. My face flooded with warmth at the term of endearment which allowed me to hope that this was perhaps about more than just sex. "I've got a vote around 4pm so I need to be in the House."

I took her foot in my hands and rubbed it softly. "Did you always want to be an MP?"

She shook her head. "No. I always felt I could make more of a difference as a lawyer."

"But that changed?" She nodded, but said no more. "And how many women get to enjoy your beautiful bathroom?" I asked playfully, trying to hide the real question – was I just another notch on the bedpost?

"Over the years there have been a few, it's true." She pouted, and scraped her wet hair away from her face. My heart sank. "But darling Cam, you're the first in a long while." She shifted, and moved forward to kiss me gently on the lips. I smiled. "And now, I really must go." I grasped the sides of the bath, readying myself to get out too. "No, you stay as long as you like. It'll be a thrill for me in my meeting knowing you are here in my bath, naked." I laughed. There was something so beautifully self-assured about Sara that made me feel calm. I laid back and watched her climb out of the bath and into a large fluffy white towel. She left the room and a few moments later reappeared in a smart black suit with a deep pink blouse underneath. Her dark hair was tied back and she quickly glanced in the mirror to put on her lipstick. "I would like to see you again, Cam, if you'd like that?"

"Yes, of course. I mean, I'd love that." I smiled broadly.

"Cute." She gave me a quick kiss and then she was gone. I laid back in the bath and closed my eyes for a moment, allowing myself to inhale the steam that swirled around me. I still wasn't sure of Sara's intentions, but I was too intoxicated by her to bring myself to care. After another 10 minutes soaking, I slowly lifted myself out of the water, and reached for my own towel. She had left one in easy reach for me. It was beautifully soft, and had warmed on the rail. I wrapped it around myself and put my feet into a pair of slippers nearby. Sara's of course. They were soft and inviting, and in them I walked around the apartment. I felt like a ghost, visiting a stranger's home, unseen, unheard.

I walked into the lounge, in which we'd spent no time this afternoon, and looked at the giant book shelves that filled one wall. I had learned a long time ago that much could be learnt from someone's bookshelf. She had many of the classic lesbian fiction novels I had read as a young woman coming to terms with my sexuality. It made me smile to think she had enjoyed those pages too. There were large coffee table books about Africa, architecture, the Middle East, black and white film. It was an eclectic collection, which provided evidence to me of a complex mind. It reassured me to know that as an MP she had books on physics, fine art, sociology and 1970s sit coms. They seemed a pretty good grounding to me in British politics. There were some more predictable offerings, biographies of Margaret Thatcher, Tony Blair, John Major and Tony Benn. She didn't discriminate. She loved a political heavyweight, from either side of the house.

I felt a shiver of secretive delight at exploring her bookshelves, as though I was reading her diary. I could easily imagine her pouring herself a glad of red wine and pulling a tome from the shelf to keep her entertained for an evening. I noticed there was no television in the room, although there was a digital radio. I switched it on. Radio 4. I could probably have predicted that. I turned it back off.

Once back in the bedroom, I rescued my clothes from the heap they'd been unceremoniously left in. I got dressed, and returned to the bathroom to do my hair. I found what looked like a makeup bag and borrowed her eyeliner. I felt that she wouldn't begrudge me a simple touch up. I looked at myself in the mirror, and smiled at my rosy cheeks. It felt good to be wanted.

I found my bag and let myself out, dropping the latch as I went. The door made a satisfying heavy thud as it closed. I wondered if I would be there again soon.

Chapter 6

Dr Smart arrived exactly on time, her clothes immaculate and her hair styled to perfection. Her brisk walk camouflaged her age. I was already in the reception area waiting for her. I didn't like to keep people waiting. She held out her hand for me. I took it and was surprised at the softness of the skin. I thought about all the many hundreds and thousands of people those hands had operated on over the years. She still had a firm grip. I welcomed her back to the college, to which she hadn't returned in several decades. Then we walked together towards the laboratory. I had already been there earlier in the morning to check that everything was ready to demonstrate to her, and that the researchers knew who she was, and what she was interested in. I'd also told them that, if things went well, there may be an outside chance of some funding.

"How are you Miss Strawbank?" she asked, as we walked to the laboratories.

"Oh, do call me Cameron, please." I smiled as she nodded formally. We went through several doors that were swipe access only – I had been afforded special privileges for the day.

"The outside of the building is the same," she said, "but the inside is so different. It bears no relation really." We walked into the clean white interior of one of the labs, where students and researchers were working with centrifuges and all manner of technical equipment. "I did a little research as part of my training," she waved her hand at all the equipment displaying digital readings, "but it's so different. The labs were all dark brown and wooden. Of course, things have moved on. This is a very good thing." We made our way to the back of the lab, which emitted a low hum of machinery and infrequent chatter, where Dr Kauser was ready for us.

"Dr Smart, please meet Dr Kauser." The two women shook hands. "Dr Kauser leads on the genetic work we discussed when we met before, and has a few things to show you to demonstrate some of her research."

"Welcome, Dr Smart," said Dr Kauser, smiling. She was a researcher through and through, naturally shy, but her eyes lit up when she spoke of her research. "Come and see the cell lines we've been working on." She ushered us into an adjoining room, which was smaller than the last. It contained incubators and fridges and all sorts of kit that I didn't recognise. Dr Kauser talked us through what she wanted to achieve, using words that I mostly understood, but only very superficially. Dr Smart though seemed to have no problem keeping up and referenced several scientific papers that Dr Kauser seemed to know well, which animated her. This was my cue to stay quiet and let the experts do their stuff. My role was purely as a facilitator.

After a while we were led to a high powered microscope, through which Dr Kauser showed us the breast cancer cells she was studying, growing, and hopefully learning how to deactivate. To me they just looked like pink blobs, but it was remarkable all the same seeing them at such close quarters and thinking about the damage they caused so many.

After 40 minutes or so Dr Kauser had to go – she had lecturing responsibilities. I got the sense from her that she would much preferred to have stayed with me and Dr Smart, telling us about her work. We said our goodbyes and Dr Smart and I left the labs.

"Do you have time for a coffee and a slice of cake?" I asked. Dr Smart gave me a knowing smile.

"I should think so. I have my cheque book, you will be pleased to know." I smiled politely. She knew where the next conversation was heading.

Knighton University College has one of the most envied campuses in the UK, with large expanses of greenery and beautiful red brick Edwardian buildings. It was inevitable however that, inside one of these buildings, there was a Costa Coffee. It seemed somewhat incongruous given the heritage of the college. That said, I suspected it was the only one with a large, shiny grand piano in it.

"Crikey," said Dr Smart as I set down her coffee and Bakewell Tart, "does anyone play that thing?"

"Not often, although at the end of term last year some of our music students hosted something of an impromptu cabaret there, which was great fun."

"Now that sounds perfect." There was a sparkle in Dr Smart's eyes. "I remember singing in a Medical School revue many moons ago. I couldn't sing a note, but that didn't hold me back - or any of the others for that matter. Me and the handful of other girls were always in demand when it came to the Christmas show each year, else it was something of a homoerotic affair. Only 10 years or so before us, they just used to have the chaps drag up to play the girl parts. Imagine that." I laughed. The changes in the college never ceased to make me think about my own route through life and the privilege I had simply by not being held back by my gender.

"It sounds like you made the most of your time here."

"Oh yes, very much. And it looks like Dr Kauser is too. What an extraordinary thing she is doing. I was very impressed. What I want to know is, what can I do to help?" Dr Smart was nothing if not practical.

"Well, I guess we have to be guided by you there. Small things, like funding an undergraduate to work in her lab over the summer break can make a difference, to bigger things like funding a PhD student over three years. The more support she has with her research, the quicker she will see results."

"But she's not going to achieve a miracle cure overnight though is she?"

"No," I said, cutting a piece off the Danish pastry I'd bought myself, "this is the first step in understanding the microbiology of the condition. Hers is a life's work. You can see how committed to it she is." Dr Smart took a sip from her coffee and we sat for a moment in companionable silence.

"What would she need for a PhD student for three years and all that goes with it?"

"About £60,000 I would say." Another silence. Dr Smart took a thoughtful bite from her Bakewell. I glanced around the room at the undergraduates who were dotted around the room, sipping elaborate coffee based drinks with cream on top, wondering if they had any idea of the difference in experience they were having in comparison to the woman in front of me.

"Ok. Let's do that for now, but I think we should talk again about the future – the future beyond me I mean. I won't live forever." Before I could thank her, she took out her cheque book and wrote out the amount. She signed it and tore it from her book, handing it to me. "There. A good afternoon's work for you I think?"

"Thank you Dr Smart, this will make a huge difference to Dr Kauser and her work. I can't wait to tell her about your generosity." Dr Smart started to organise her belongings, and put her jacket on. "Can I walk you to your car?"

"If you like," she said in a way that assured me that she would be perfectly fine if I didn't. A few minutes later we were standing beside a large black Bentley. We said our goodbyes, and then she hopped in and drove off. I was left in her wake, trying to imagine what she was like 60 years before. I started to walk back to the office and contemplated what I would be like at her age. I couldn't picture myself there. An old sadness tugged at my thoughts. I had never been able to imagine myself as an old person. I thrust my hands into my pockets and looked at my feet taking one step at a time.

"You look thoughtful," said Tom, as I took a seat at my desk.

"Hmmm," I said absently.

"How did the meeting go?" I suddenly recalled the success I'd experienced over a Bakewell Tart. I smiled, and then walked up to the whiteboard on which we would write up our successful gift pledges. Tom and a few of my colleagues paused, watching expectantly. I wrote Dr Smart's name, followed by her donation. A small cheer went up. "That deserves a double choc chip cookie my dear," said Tom, rustling in his drawer for the special biscuits he only broke out for a five figure gift. I wasn't sure what he rewarded his colleagues with for a six figure gift, but a cookie suited me and kept the smile on my face for another ten minutes.

A few moments later an email bounced into my inbox with a line in the header that simply read "fancy a weekend in the country?" I felt my cheeks redden. There was nothing else in the main text of the email, except for the name – Sara.

Tom and I went to the staff bar after work. "Congratulations darling," said Tom, as we clinked our beer glasses together. "A good day's work."

"A good day all round really. Sara's just invited me for a weekend away in the country."

"Oooh la la! A dirty weekend. I like it."

In mock effrontery I humphed and then laughed. "I'm sure we'll have intellectual discussions too."

"Oh yes, it'll be all Chaucer and Chomsky I can tell…" He rolled his eyes. "Bloody lesbians, you can't just call a spade a spade can you?"

"Maybe it's more than just a spade?"

"Oh hello," said Tom, raising his eyebrows, "are you getting attached? Does this mean you're over Hayley?"

"Maybe. I bumped into her the other day actually."

"I hope you didn't let her make you feel like a lost puppy."

"No," I said, knowing that it was a lie.

"She didn't deserve you. I haven't decided about the MP yet. I'll wait until I meet her." He drained his glass.

"As if I'll let you meet her. You're a liability." I ordered another drink, shaking my head at him.

"Harsh. I only have your best interests at heart Cam, and you know it. Besides, who else am I going to live vicariously through?" I laughed at him. "Seriously though darling, I'm pleased for you. Be careful though. You deserve someone who'll be good to you."

"Don't we all?" He waggled his head in agreement.

"Hello there, fancy seeing you both here!" Tom and I turned in surprise. It was Damien. "Can I get you a drink?" We pointed at our nearly full glasses. He nodded and went over to the bar.

"Oh God, he's going to invite himself to join us isn't he?" said Tom under his breath. I smiled sweetly, feeling the same as Tom.

"Do you mind?" said Damien, as he pulled up a chair at their table.

"Be my guest," I said.

"Oh heavens, is that the time?" said Tom, looking at his watch, "so sorry chaps, I have to dash – Mrs de Winter needs feeding." I shot him daggers as he downed the remainder of his drink in two gulps, while pulling his jacket on. "Toodleoo, see you tomorrow." He knew that I knew that his cat would be unlikely to be anywhere near his flat for another few hours.

Damien laughed. "That Tom, he's a card!" I smiled weakly. I would be having words with Tom later. "I actually wanted to take the opportunity to congratulate you, Cameron, you've had a great few weeks. Two five figure gifts, and both from new donors. Fantastic work."

"Ah, thanks Damien. That's kind of you to say."

"No, it's not kindness Cameron, it's the truth. You've really upped your game in the last few weeks. It's impressive to see. It just goes to show that all the hard work is worth it." He looked meaningfully at me in a way that made my skin prickle.

"I've had a couple of lucky breaks, it'll be someone else next week."

"Don't brush it off. You've shown real skill. It's not luck, it's all down to you and our team." He took a swig from his bottle of beer. "It just goes to show that we all need to be ABC."

"Hmm?"

"Always be closing!" He grinned. "Two big gifts from two new donors. Tell me about Sara Lorenzo – we've been trying to get through her front door for a couple of years, but she's always resisted. I never really thought she'd bite. But she really did, didn't she?"

"Um, yes, I suppose so," I dipped my nose into my glass and took a sip.

"The darling of the champagne socialist elite, and you managed to get her talking. You'll have to tell me your tricks." I smiled sweetly, and felt a droplet of sweat drip down my back. I had avoided thinking about the implications of my relationship with Sara in terms of my professional role. "So, tell me about your cultivation strategy for her. Are you planning to see her again?"

My cheeks went hot as I thought about the forthcoming weekend in the country, which I suspected didn't fall within the Fundraiser's Book of Handy Hints. "Well, I thought I'd see if she wanted to come to the House of Lords."

"Nice touch Cameron, yes, we can make a bit of a fuss of her. At least it will be nice and local for her – just next door." Damien laughed at his joke. I smiled again, taking another, bigger gulp of my drink. I couldn't imagine Sara taking to Damien 'making a fuss' of her.

"Yes. I've invited Dr Smart as well."

"Good legacy prospect there I should say – knocking on 90 isn't she?" I felt slightly offended by Damien's words. Dr Smart felt like so much more than an age on a database. She had more to offer than a fat cheque in a will.

"We'll see."

"Well, keep it up. You're really looking like you're going places, definitely one to watch for me," he said, tapping the side of his nose with his index finger. At that moment his phone bleeped. He looked down, and snapped his head back up. "Dammit, sorry, gotta go. The Mrs wants me to do bath time with the twins tonight." He necked his beer and disappeared from the bar as quickly as he'd appeared.

I breathed out. It was a relief to see him go, but his words 'cultivation strategy' kept going round in my head. I sat back in my seat and sent a message to Sara, confirming that a weekend in the country sounded exactly what I wanted to do. I could talk to her about how we managed her donations and the professional side of things then.

Later that evening I called Sara. "Hi Cam, lovely to hear your voice, how was your day?"

I smiled, hearing her own smile in her voice. "Good thanks. Spent a couple of hours with a remarkable woman."

"Oh hello, and I thought I was the only woman in your life," said Sara. I could almost hear the twinkle in her eye.

"This one's got a few years on you, a few decades even. You'd love her – a pioneering surgeon of her time."

"You get to meet all the interesting people."

"Says you. Who did you meet today?" I asked.

"Oh, local surgery darling, I met a woman who is fed up with the council leaving her wheelie bin on the wrong side of the road, and a chap who is convinced the Queen is an FBI agent." I laughed. An MP's life wasn't always as glamorous as people imagined.

"Sounds thrilling."

"Not nearly as thrilling as this weekend will be."

"Oh yes," I said, "where are we going?"

"Not telling. Pick you up at 6 on Friday?"

"From home?"

"Yes. That ok?"

"Sure," I said uncertainly. I suddenly felt self-conscious about my own modest flat in comparison with her lavish apartment. Somehow, meeting her in London when we'd seen each other so far allowed it to feel unreal. Bringing her into my world felt a lot more of a risk.

"You haven't got a secret girlfriend tucked away there have you?" she asked teasingly.

"Ha ha, no. Just me, a messy kitchen and a pile of newspapers. Looking forward to it."

"Fabulous. I can't wait."

I felt a small thrill at the sense that we may spend a whole night together, wake up together, eat breakfast together. Like a couple might.

Chapter 7

The next morning it was with a heavy heart that I walked into the team meeting. It irked me that it was termed a 'team meeting' rather than a staff meeting like it would any other day. I knew this would be management bingo central. The only bright point on the horizon was the knowledge that Tom would position himself opposite me across the table, so we could have an eyebrow discussion throughout. We would allow ourselves the occasional eye roll, but tried to keep it to a minimum in case someone saw.

I walked into the room and saw a Powerpoint slide with a complicated graph projected onto the wall. I felt my insides sag, and helped myself to some coffee. I glanced to my left, where Tom was doing the same. With a totally straight face he was getting himself two cups.

"These blessed cups are far too small," he said, before stalking off, nose in the air. I took my customary seat opposite him, and after a bit of paper shuffling, and checking of laser pointers, Damien called the meeting to order.

"So, this is our chance to touch base, exchange ideas, and indulge in a bit of blue sky thinking." I gazed into my coffee, trying not to smirk too obviously. "The year is going well, and we are on track to hit our target, but let's be clear, it won't just happen. We've all got to seize the moment, and get closing those gifts." Damien turned to the slide, and used one of his pointers to demonstrate where on our donation trajectory we were as an organisation. I squinted to see the detail in amongst the complex charts, lines, data points and superfluous information. "I know this is a bit busy, but you can see that we are in exactly the position that we need to be in. But, as they say, if you reach for the moon, you might just reach the stars. So let's all have a look at our pipelines – who can give us an extra few grand? Who can add a nought to the end of their donation?"

I swallowed a grimace as I looked at Tom, exchanging furrowed brows with him. I felt annoyed by the words being used. They didn't match up to my experiences – not with Dr Smart, or Sara. Although of course, Sara was another matter. I frowned and pretended to study my notepad. If this really was to turn into a genuine relationship, what would that mean for my job?

"Now, " continued Damien, bringing up another slide that was far too complex to make any meaningful sense, "as you can see here, I have used this slide to show how each of you have contributed so far to our total to date." I looked around the table to see bowed heads, people scribbling down information. I was intrigued as to what they were scribbling – we all knew our own numbers, although we didn't necessarily know each other's.

It was a long morning, of discussions about the 'plumbing' of exceeding our target, as Damien described it. By the time lunchtime came I was ready for a break. My phone vibrated in my pocket as the meeting drew to a close. It was a text from Tom. I looked up to see him looking nonchalantly at the final slide of Damien's presentation.

//Fancy a cheeky glass of red? Meet you at the Dog in five x//

I caught his eye briefly, and nodded.

"And finally," said Damien, "I just wanted to say well done to Cameron. She's been putting all of this fantastic theory into practice and making things happen. First a five figure gift from Sara Lorenzo MP, and now a significant donation from Dr Smart. It really does show that if you kiss enough frogs, you get a prince now and again." I blushed, not expecting the compliment. I was also slightly perturbed by his turn of phrase. I didn't class either Dr Smart or Sara a frog.

Tom was waiting at the bar for me. It was a pub just off campus, where we were less likely to bump into Damien or any of his cronies. He had ordered a couple of glasses of wine, so we found a table in a quiet corner. "So, Cam, kissed any frogs recently?" I glared at him.

"Nope. She didn't turn into a prince either," I took a sip of wine, "thank God."

"Yes, that really would have been embarrassing." He smiled. "You ok? You seemed to be frowning a lot in there. I know Damien's an utter bore, but you seemed even more miserable than usual for a team meeting."

I sighed. "I suppose I'm just a bit worried about this whole business with Sara."

"What, your dirty weekend?" I laughed.

"No, not that. I just wonder about the wisdom of seeing someone who has made such a big donation. Can you imagine what would happen if someone were to find out. It could be seriously misunderstood."

"But how would anyone find out?"

"Oh come on, Tom, you know what this place is like, it's a hotbed of gossip. She made the donation before anything happened, but the only people who know that are the two of us." Tom thought for a moment before speaking.

"What do you think you should do?"

"That's the thing, I don't know. I don't even know if this is anything beyond a bit of fun for her." I looked glumly into the bottom of my glass.

"You want it to be more?" Tom asked.

"I think so. I don't know. I like her, I do. But we live in different places, we live different lives, she's older than me... But when we're together, we just, it just…"

"It just doesn't matter," he finished for me. "You're scared of getting hurt, Strawbank." I frowned, but then allowed myself a nod.

"None of which helps in terms of what I do about what is, essentially, an ethical dilemma."

"Ok, hun, leave it with me. I'll come up with a plausible reason to palm prospecting duties for Sara off on someone else."

"Thanks Tom, I owe you one." We finished our wine, and then walked back to the office.

6pm on Friday eventually arrived. Just afterwards the buzzer to my apartment rang. I sprang to my feet, which were in the third pair of shoes I'd tried on. I wanted to look casual but stylish for our journey to wherever we were going. I rolled my eyes at myself. Then I picked up the entry phone.

"It's me, let me in, I want to see the place!" came Sara's excited voice, distorted slightly by the cheap electronic system. I pressed the entry key and heard the door downstairs open and then shut. A few seconds later I heard her knuckles rap on my door firmly. I felt anxiety, apprehension, excitement and joy hit me all at once before I went to the door to open it. I tried to affect a relaxed smile, but I suspect I failed.

"Hi, gorgeous girl, how are you?" she asked, kissing me full on the lips, before walking in. "You look lovely. Love those shoes." She glanced at my holdall in the corner of the lounge. "First I want the guided tour, and then we need to hit the road."

I took her round my modest apartment. It was small and perfectly formed. A bit messy in places, but it was my home. "I suppose you might call it bijou," I said, popping a lock of hair behind my ear.

"Actually, I'd call it perfect." Sara smiled, and the muscles in my shoulders relaxed. "Let's go." She took my hand and it wasn't long before we were in her car – a racing green sports car.

"Midlife crisis car?" I asked, giggling.

"Charming! I've had this for years!" She laughed and switched on some music. For a time we didn't speak, just listened to the beat pulsing through the expensive speakers. I lost myself in the movement, the journey, the buildings we were passing. There was something meditative about it. Sara's eyes remained on the road, her hands smoothly steering and changing gear, at one with the vehicle. I still had no clue where we were going, but we were heading north.

It was an hour or so into the journey that the spell was broken. Sara's smooth voice was a welcome interruption. "So, Cam, what's your story?"

"What do you mean?"

"Well, we all have one don't we? That one moment that changes you, makes you who you are."

"What makes you think I'm that interesting?"

"Oh darling, I know you are that interesting. Your depths are somewhat opaque." I smiled, and closed my eyes. I was making a show of thinking. She was of course right. I stalled.

"What's your story then?" I asked. Sara raised her eyebrows and gave a wry smile.

"I see. Ok, my story." She indicated and looked over her shoulder as she changed lanes. "Well, I married my best friend. Matthew."

"Man Matthew?"

"Control yourself! Yes, man Matthew. A very lovely man too. I met him at university. We studied together and just understood each other right from the start."

"Didn't you know you were gay?"

"Well, I guess so, on some level. But it was just easier. We liked each other, we had fun together. There was no pressure, no jealousy."

"No passion…"

"Passion's not everything!" I raised my eyebrows. "OK, so perhaps it is important," she touched my knee before going on, "but we were young. We didn't know ourselves." I opened my mouth to speak. "No, I don't mean about the gay thing. Obviously that was a factor – not just for me. He was someone to hold on to. My parents died when I was in my late teens – they had me later in life, and both succumbed to cancer within 12 months of each other. Matthew was security." I nodded. There was no trace of pity in her voice.

"What happened?"

"We married the summer we graduated. We moved out of the shared house we were in with our friends and started married life. It was a bit of a game. We had a small wedding, all we could afford really, and spent a week on the Costa del Sol."

"Classy!"

"We thought so! We spent most of the time drinking cocktails and fending off hangovers."

"And did you…"

"And did we what?" She moved into the outside lane to overtake. "Oh, I see. Yes, of course, he was my husband." I raised my eyebrows. "Are you telling me you're a gold star, Strawbank?" I blushed. "Heavens. Bless your little lesbian heart!"

I laughed. "I had the opportunity, but never the motivation. I never really saw the point of sex until I met my first girlfriend." I chewed the inside of my cheek.

"Well it certainly wasn't a significant feature of the honeymoon – more of a drunken afterthought."

"And then what happened?"

"Then we came home and started our adult lives together. It was all a bit of an anti-climax. Somehow I thought that our carefree student lives would continue just as they used to, but job hunting, working 9 to 5 and the mundane was quite a comedown."

"Yeah, there's something a bit real about graduating and becoming a proper grown up." Sara smiled sadly. She pulled into the slip road towards a service station. She continued her tale over coffee.

"We muddled through for a while, but, as they say, reality bites. He met someone, I met someone, and after a while it became clear that we would both probably live happily ever after as friends rather than spouses."

"Did you tell him? That you were gay I mean?"

"I didn't really need to. He walked in on me having sex with my then girlfriend one afternoon. I think we'd both been in denial until then, but after that we couldn't ignore it. We saw a solicitor the following week."

"That all sounds rather dramatic," I said, recalling the dramas of my own late teens.

"Actually, it wasn't so much. We had only ever really been friends. Like I say – no jealousy."

"Do you still have contact?"

"Oh yes," she said, smiling broadly, "I see him for lunch quite regularly. He went travelling after we divorced, and a few months later came back with an Australian girl. He married her a couple of years later. They've got two daughters now and are very happy. I'm their fairy godmother." I laughed. It sounded more than amicable.

"So where are we going then? Are you going to tell me now?" Sara laughed, making me want to kiss her.

"Well, if you haven't guessed already, it'll become pretty obvious soon. We're heading towards the Lake District where I've got a cosy cottage waiting for us."

"Now that sounds perfect."

It was perfect. It was dark by the time we arrived, but we walked into a beautifully laid out living room, complete with flowers and champagne, and a wood burning stove all set up and ready to go. I stowed my bag in the small but elegant bedroom, and found Sara poking about in the stove. "I'll open the bubbles then shall I?"

"No, I've got a better idea, you light this bloody thing, and I'll do the bolly!" She handed me a box of matches and we switched. There was something idyllic about the place, as though we had been transported into a different world. Jazz was playing on the stereo – something I never usually had time for, but this evening it was perfect.

Between us we rustled up steak and chips thanks to the rather well stocked pantry at the cottage – perhaps she really was a fairy godmother. The food, the drink, the candlelight, the warmth of the fire, all served to make her yet more irresistible. Her perfectly shaped mouth laughed and talked and smiled and ate and drank, and it wasn't long before we were in bed, wrapped in a slow and passionate grip. I no longer cared how many times she had rehearsed this seduction, or whether I was special. All I could see and feel was her and it mattered little how I felt tomorrow, or next week or next month. Clothes and jewellery were strewn across the room, falling where they were flung. A champagne flute was on its side on the bedside cabinet, fizzing spots of liquid surrounding it. Nothing else mattered, just her.

Hours later we lay, exhausted but happy. Sara was absently running a finger along the length of my ear. "So darling, what's your story? I told you mine, but somehow you got out of telling yours."

"Well," I said slowly, "I met this crazy passionate extravagant woman once, who whisked me to a mountain idyll and ravished me..." I giggled as she tickled me.

"Come on, Cam, I know so little of you. There's so much there isn't there? You don't share so much. Am I just another notch on your bedpost?"

"On my bedpost?" I lifted my head in surprise. "You can't really believe that can you?"

"Well, what else am I?" There was a laugh in her voice, but seriousness in her eyes. "You're busy keeping yourself safe and far away from me. I wonder sometimes what you're afraid of."

"Well, I promise you, you're not a notch." I pulled a sheet over my naked torso. "You're a gorgeous adventure. I'm not. I've never been. Perhaps there's nothing more to tell."

"For the record, Cam, you're more than a notch too. You wanted to ask that too didn't you?" said Sara. I looked down. "You should have just asked. I don't know what this is, but I like it." I smiled and felt myself go red. "If you won't tell me your story, then you'll have to permit me to ask you a series of personal questions."

"Oh God. I need another drink if you're going to do this," I said, hopping out of bed and rescuing the overturned glass. I poured us both a drink and awaited my fate.

"Your first love."

I took a breath.

"Caroline Parker." I felt my fists clench of their own accord.

"And?" she wasn't going to let me off easily.

"We met at university, in freshers week of course."

"Love at first sight?"

"No. I thought she seemed rather frumpy actually. She wore these dreadful floaty flowery skirts and wore her hair in an unflattering bob. Well, that was my first impression." I sighed. "I knew I was probably gay, but I'd never done anything about it. Somehow, within a couple of weeks we became inseparable. We were friends, but it meant more. So much more than something as tawdry as sex, or sexuality. She was my world."

"Did she feel the same?"

"I didn't think so. For six months we had what I would now describe as an ambiguous friendship. There was a lot of late night talking, hand holding, accidentally falling asleep together." I used air quotes for the last bit. "I became a master at calling on her in her room at the perfect moment to be able to legitimately stay for a while and watch something dire on telly and drop off. I'd wake with her arm draped over me, as she casually ate another custard cream from the packet we'd have devoured most of earlier in the evening. Once she even fell asleep too. I awoke with her breath on my face. The sort of thing that would now make me want to turn my head immediately, but there was something adolescent and obsessive about my love for Caroline. I breathed her in."

"It sounds positively Victorian! There's a lot of literature charting 'romantic friendships' between women during that period. Lots of hand holding and heaving bosoms. Did yours heave?"

"Oh I think so. Quite often, especially when I thought she wasn't looking." I laughed. "Of course, I was nowhere near as subtle as I imagined I was being. I would spend pained evenings alone in my room agonising over this great love and my urges to kiss her, feeling I was somehow betraying her purity of soul."

"Good God, that really is Victorian." I smirked, remembering the exquisite pain of it. Somehow it was the kind of thing you only did once. For me anyway.

"She became more important than anything else. All my friends tired of hearing about her, and my parents simply assumed I was having an affair with her and left me to it. They didn't tell me that until afterwards though. There's something about first love I think – you really do feel like you are the only person in the world who has ever felt it, like no one else could ever understand the passion, the pain, the enormity."

"You're such an old romantic aren't you?" Sara smiled, and put a protective arm around me. She kissed me tenderly and urged me to go on.

"One day we were sitting in her room, watching her telly, lying side by side on her single bed, as we always did. She turned her head to find me looking at her. The bob that I had poo-pooed before was high fashion and I couldn't take my eyes off her skin. I immediately went red, caught in the act. But instead of looking away, or looking shocked, she simply said, 'You know, you could just kiss me.'"

"Heavens! What did you do?" I laughed at the memory and told Sara what happened next. I had been so shocked that I leapt out of bed and immediately said that of course I didn't want to do that because it would be dishonourable.

"I might cease to be perfect, Cameron," said Caroline that evening, "but it won't be dishonourable. You want to kiss me, I want to kiss you and I just think we should do it."

"But you are perfect to me," I said.

"I know sweetie. That's why I haven't said anything before. I don't want to fall off the pedestal you've put me on. I'm just ordinary."

"Oh God, you could never be anything but wildly extraordinary," I declared through dramatic tears. And then I did kiss her. I don't remember much of what followed, but the following weeks passed in a haze of the pure addiction of passion, romance and sex. Looking back, it seemed almost chemical.

"And did she fall from her pedestal?" Asked Sara, looking at me curiously. I shook my head, and then nodded.

"I guess she did. In a way." I took a big swallow of champagne. "We were together for six months. We told our parents – neither set was at all shocked or surprised by the announcement given how inseparable we'd been before that. It was one Friday night, we were due to go out together." I felt my fists clench again. "She didn't want to come. She'd had an awful cough all week and her asthma was playing up. I'd been on at her all week to go to the doctor so she'd start getting better and maybe be able to come to the party with me. One of our friends was turning 21 and was hosting a house party. Anyway, she was tired and feeling a bit rubbish, so with a heavy heart I left her behind."

"And Cinders went to the ball?" said Sara with a smile on her face. "And misbehaved?"

"I got there and there was this girl who I'd seen around campus. We flirted a little, and for the first time I thought of an existence beyond Caroline. I suppose I was curious about being with someone else. I don't even remember what she looked like, but we talked for hours. I had promised to get in by 11 and say goodnight to Caroline."

"But you didn't?" I shook my head.

"Time seemed irrelevant that evening. I don't know why. I was having fun. I was beginning to see how life would be to be attracted to someone without being tortured by the sense that they were perfect, or that I shouldn't say anything. I didn't do anything."

"But?"

"But nothing. I didn't do anything. I caught the night bus back to my halls of residence." Immediately I could recall in detail the blue flashing lights I'd seen as I got off the bus, the smell of exhaust fumes in the air, the dull murmur of pale-faced students. Some poor soul was being loaded into the back of an ambulance, and I could see the warden climbing in behind. It must have been about 2am. Before I could see any more, the ambulance drove off into the dark. I walked towards Caroline's room. I would sneak in and kiss her goodnight, to assuage some of the guilt I felt at coming home so late and flirting with someone else. I had spent the whole bus journey battling with my conscience. I felt I should tell her what I had done. But then again, what had I done? I'd had a conversation. But somehow that felt like a disingenuous description. I walked slowly down her corridor, telling myself again and again I'd done nothing wrong. When I got to her door it was open. I didn't understand. I knew she was going to have an early night, why would she still be up? A dark fear built inside me, and before I even looked into the room I knew it would be empty.

Sara still had her arm around me. "It had been her in the ambulance. She had a massive asthma attack. The only way she could get help was by banging on the wall and waking the girl in the room next door. She called an ambulance straight away when she saw the state Caroline was in. She was in a bad way when they put her in the ambulance. She died that night." A warm tear dropped onto my cheek.

"Christ, you poor thing." Sara kissed my cheek gently, almost respectfully, as though I wasn't there with her, but with someone else.

"I won't rehearse the what-ifs with you here and now. But there are many of them. They have dulled with time, but if things had even been a little different, she may have lived." I took in a deep medicinal breath, and drained my glass.

"You feel guilty?"

"Sometimes. Less now than I did. It feels more like a fairy tale now than real life. A perfect love gone too soon."

"Perfection is a dangerous thing," said Sara gently.

"I know, I've been told that before."

The next morning we donned our waterproofs and headed out onto the wind ravaged landscape, the elements clearing my head of the previous night's confessions.

Chapter 8

It was a few weeks later I found myself on a coach to London. Damien was grilling me from across the aisle about my gift pipeline, and getting me to list the key individuals I would be targeting this evening at the House of Lords. I could feel Tom, who was in the window seat beside me, jabbing me in the ribs.

"So tell me more about Sara Lorenzo, Cameron, do you think we'll see her this evening?" asked Damien, who was fiddling with his lapel pin as he spoke.

I grabbed Tom's finger, determined not to giggle as I responded. "Unfortunately not tonight. There's a late debate and vote in the Commons, so she has sent her apologies."

"Hmmm, shame, I wanted to meet that woman." Damien looked genuinely disappointed. I smiled ruefully. I was, in a way, relieved that she wouldn't be there. "I had to persuade Tom not to move her onto another team member. He seems to think that one of the more junior staff might work with her well, to give them experience, and you a bit more capacity." I felt Tom's finger, that I was still gripping, tense. "I don't think it's a good idea. If you want something done, ask a busy person. You're having a purple patch, let's keep it up." I released Tom's finger, confident he wouldn't jab me anymore. I wasn't sure what to say. I smiled and nodded. I grabbed the research papers for the event and made the appearance of looking at them. Damien turned to his own sheaf. I exhaled. My mobile vibrated.

//Sorry honey, I tried xx//

It was from Tom, who was looking out of the window. He turned and gave me an apologetic glance before looking back out of the window.

//No worries, we'll muddle through. You owe me a sneaky glass of red tonight though x//

Tom smirked as he read the text. Technically we were all banned from drinking during these events, in order to stay on top of things. I looked at the research pack, which included mug shots and brief bios of all the guests. It was a handy reference guide of interests, recent and forthcoming donations and useful gems – for example one or two of the prospects had a coded note basically advising serious conversations to happen towards the beginning to the night due to their tendency to have a few too many drinks at these events. There was one guest in particular who had a sad face after his bio. I knew that this was Tom's code to advise all female staff to avoid this prospect once he'd had a glass or two of wine due to wandering hands. I planned to stay away from him altogether. Nothing is worth getting groped for.

We arrived at the imposing building, and filed into the entrance we were directed to, going through airport style security and posing for a photo so pixelated it seemed pointless printing it and putting it on our guest lanyards. We gathered our possessions and processed down narrow corridors to an elegant suite which overlooked the Thames. The events team swung into action, setting up the reception desk, and Damien pulled the fundraisers together for a last minute pep talk. This could be summarised with a series of phrases that wouldn't be out of place in yet another game of management jargon bingo. I slunk towards the back and checked my phone surreptitiously.

//Hi darling, sorry I can't make it tonight. Bloody democracy! Bleed'em dry… S x//

The brief message made my pulse quicken, and I felt excitement ping in my chest in the knowledge she was only a few hundred yards away from me – albeit through several security cordons, which I would never be able to get through, even with my pixelated security pass.

"Welcome, welcome," said a well-spoken elderly gentleman who had seemingly wandered in from nowhere.

"Ah," said Damien, swelling with pride, "this is Lord Stannington, he is our generous host this evening." An alumnus of the college, he was our 'door opener' as Damien would have it.

"Thank you, Damien, a pleasure to see you all here. It is a delight to once again host the college in this wonderful venue. Do please enjoy your evening, and let us hope that our guests will be inspired to donate."

None of us knew how much Lord Stannington had donated. We knew he did, and regularly, but he preferred to remain anonymous. He gave the general impression of being what my Gran would call 'a good egg' and was what Damien would call 'old money'.

We were sent on our way with a metaphorical pat on the head just as the early guests began to arrive. Dr Smart was bang on time, which surprised me not one bit. She arrived, unruffled, asking where she might safely stow her coat and bag. I exchanged her belongings with a glass of orange juice, at her request, and took her over to the window to enjoy the view.

"I always think there is a certain romance about the Thames," I said, unable to put Sara out of my mind, and the alternative night we might be having if she were free and I wasn't working.

"I always thought it was a grey, smelly, ugly thing," said Dr Smart with a laugh, "but to each their own." It was a good natured jab, and reminded me of why I liked the woman before me, dressed in a well-tailored trouser suit. A moment later she spotted someone she knew, and vanished into the crowd that had begun to gather.

Waiters were bringing round red and white wine and stylish nibbles. I was tucking into a mini Yorkshire pudding with roast beef in as I bumped into Martin Lockwood. I smiled apologetically as I rapidly chewed my mouthful. "Well this," said Martin, smiling at me generously, "is seriously impressive. How on earth did you get this place?" I swallowed the last of the food before I spoke.

"Excuse me, sorry. With the House of Lords I'm afraid it's all about who you know. Lord Stannington over there, he's one of our alumni – like yourself. He very kindly makes the arrangements every year and lets it all happen." I gestured towards the Lord, who was wearing a suit that I imagined almost certainly came from Savile Row. He was old money after all...

"Well, if you can call in a favour like that, then you definitely should."

"I can introduce you later if you like," I offered, waving away a waiter offering micro fish and chips. I had learnt my lesson. I felt an unexpected hand on my shoulder.

"Ah, Miss Strawbank I presume?" I turned to see Sir Hugh, holding a wine glass that was already empty. A waiter subtly replaced it with a glass of red. I smiled.

"Sir Hugh, always a pleasure. Perhaps I can introduce you to Martin Lockwood?" The men shook hands and I left them to become acquainted. I went over to the reception table to grab a glass of juice, struggling through the ever growing throng. For those of us working, there was never anything remotely relaxing about this date in our annual calendar. There was a need to appear to be the life and soul of the party, while networking and connecting like mad, and if possible moving potential donors closer to their destination – gift city. It was about saying thank you too. I had a list of people I'd noted down on my phone that I wanted to catch up with to thank them for their generosity in time or money in the last 12 months. There were only 15 or so, but with such a big crowd, it wouldn't be easy. Tom was handing out name tags to the last few guests, and I mouthed a quick, "Everything ok?" in his direction. He nodded, and gestured that he hadn't forgotten about the glass of wine he'd promised me. I grinned, and took a walk over to the terrace that the suite led out to. The warmth of so many bodies made me crave a bit of fresh air. There were of course others admiring the evening view across central London, but the atmosphere was more laid back, with one or two people having a quiet moment with a cigarette, as well as small groups of people chatting and catching up about 'old times' – something that went hand in hand with an alumni event.

I looked across the inky water which broke up the orange lights reflected in it, breathing in the river scent, which managed to be both musty and fresh. I knew the waters below were filthy, but somehow that added to their allure. The Thames was the life blood of London. A waiter offered me a glass of red wine and, once I'd checked for Damien, I took one and slipped into the shadows to have a drink. I suspected Tom had sent him. I smiled into the darkness, pleased that no one could see me, or indeed read my thoughts. I didn't know when I would next see Sara, but I was confident it would be soon. Some of the anxiety of those early weeks had died down, leaving me to revel in the glow of the early days of a fledgling relationship. The days when everything is perfect, and all contact sexually charged. I vowed to enjoy the phase while it lasted, coming as close to throwing caution to the wind as I had ever done. Was the stirring inside me love? I gulped down more wine. I had no idea. The scientist in me knew I was simply a mess of chemicals and hormones, creating lust, love and desire. But nothing really explained the way she made time stand still, acting as a muffler for the rest of the world. When we were together it really was as if nothing else existed. I watched a tug boat glide by gracefully. A cloud of cigarette smoke wafted past and I drained my glass. I knew I shouldn't stay long or I would be missed.

I reluctantly walked back into the room, which was a hubbub of voices, glass clinks and laughter. The smell of wine made me want another glass, but I knew it would be foolhardy to have another. I spotted Dr Smart sitting alone on one of the few chairs dotted around the edge of the room. I strolled over. "How's your evening, Dr Smart?"

"Lovely thank you, Cameron. There are so many people aren't there?"

"Yes, it's all a bit overwhelming really isn't it?"

"Yes, a little. There aren't too many folks of my graduation year though are there?"

"I suppose not. Do you find that hard?" I pulled up a chair and sat next to her. She shook her head.

"No, not really. It's the sort of situation that only arises if you are lucky enough to live this long. It would be churlish to complain." She gave a little laugh and pulled an elegant handkerchief from her pocket. She dabbed her forehead.

"Are you ok? Shall I fetch you some water?"

"Oh I'm fine. Just a little warm and tired. Chilled water might be quite nice though." I rested my hand on her shoulder for a moment, before going over to the doorway that led to the kitchen. Iced water was the least I could do for this woman. There were some prospects that meant more than others, and I was growing fond of Dr Smart.

"There you are," I said on my return, "can I get you anything else? You know if you wanted to sit somewhere cooler, there is a wonderful view on the terrace – in spite of your dislike of the river." Dr Smart decided that was a fine idea, so I pointed her in the right direction before heading over to Martin once more. Sir Hugh was still bending his ear and he was beginning to look like he needed rescuing.

"Sir Hugh," I said, as I approached the pair. There was a look of grateful relief on Martin's face. "Tell me what you've been up to this week." Martin smiled politely and then appeared to recognise an old friend and vanished. The things I did for my job.

"Dear girl, it's been a pretty good week. I dined with Lady Hanson-du-Bungay last night. She's a charming sort. Quite a looker in her time too." He took a gulp from his wine glass. "These things make you terribly thirsty. That fellow had me talking away for ages, I thought I'd never get away." I smiled and sipped the mineral water I had swiped from a passing waiter. "Always good to be here again – it's the best event on the calendar you chaps put on you know." He rummaged around in his jacket pocket and found an envelope. He thrust it into my hand, blustering that I shouldn't say anything and no thanks were required. It was just at that moment I felt a hand on my shoulder, stirring me from the slightly tipsy Sir

Hugh's antics. "Ah now," said Sir Hugh, locking eyes with the person who had just approached. I looked up and silently gasped. "Miss Strawbank, I really need to introduce you to this rather fabulous woman."

Sara stepped forward to join our conversation and took my hand, a twinkle in her eye, as she said: "Miss Strawbank, a pleasure to meet you. I'm Sara Lorenzo." I blushed.

"Lovely to meet you," I stammered.

"Shouldn't you be next door young lady?" said Sir Hugh, in mock judgement.

"Well, I thought I would have to be, but the vote took place sooner than I expected, so I thought I would pop through. What a marvellous surprise to see you here, Sir Hugh."

"Yes, it has been rather a while hasn't it? But I guess you champagne socialists find yourselves gallivanting around all over the place." Sara laughed at his words good humouredly.

"I suppose so, although of course it is rare we're not nursing bolly-induced hangovers," she deadpanned. I smothered a giggle and tried to avoid eye contact.

"So, Sara, how is it you come to know Sir Hugh here?" I asked, sucking in my cheeks.

"Ah well, Sir Hugh and I are political adversaries of sorts, and from time to time find ourselves at the same meetings. Often on opposite sides of the table though."

"I think you and Sara would get along splendidly, Miss Strawbank, she's got plenty of guts like you." I laughed politely.

"I think you might be right Sir Hugh," said Sara, who brought her hand up to my lapel and drew a finger down it. "Beautiful suit, Miss Strawbank. I love the colour, it brings out your eyes." Sir Hugh chuckled, as I felt a rush of excitement and the threat of a blush. I turned to place my water glass back onto a passing tray. As I returned to the duo Sara gave me a wink and pressed a glass of wine into my hand.

"Gosh," I said quietly, "if my boss comes over one of you might have to hide me – I'm not technically supposed to drink here!"

"What? Ridiculous. Money saving? Or is he trying to keep you on point for all that money you raise?" Sir Hugh said. I shook my head. He carried on. "You know, Sara, you need to be careful of this one, she'll have all the change up from down the back of your sofa and you'll be writing her cheques willy-nilly. She has a very intriguing effect on people."

"I can imagine," said Sara, still maintaining an ice cool exterior in spite of the overwhelming closeness of the room. With that I thought again of Dr Smart. Thrilling though this game was, I wanted to check she was ok on the terrace.

"I really must excuse myself for a moment – one of your fellow alumna calls." I nodded and then strolled away, aware of both Sir Hugh and Sara watching me as I left. It gave me an odd sense of confidence. I felt taller as I strode through the crowd to the fresh breeze of the terrace. On first glance I couldn't see Dr Smart. In fact, the terrace had emptied. The Vice Chancellor of the college had arrived and was calling on everyone to join him in the main room. It was speech time. I inwardly shrugged my shoulders and turned to return to the melee. It was at that point that I saw a pair of legs crookedly arranged by the wall. I started, before walking over to investigate. The sensible shoes were familiar, and once my eyes were used to the shadow cast by the wall, I knew it was Dr Smart. She looked peaceful, if crumpled, on the floor. Her skin like paper, in folds where her neck and arms were awkwardly folded. I called her name but there was no response. I tried to sit her up but she was completely unconscious and almost impossible to move.

"Dr Smart, Dr Smart, it's me, Cameron. Are you ok?" I held tight to one of her hands, which was cold. I checked she was breathing and was relieved to feel the faintest breath emerge from her mouth. Her pulse was there but I knew nothing else beyond that. I looked over my shoulder. Still no one. I could hear the horn of a boat passing and the applause of the speech inside. I had to make a choice – either leave her, or shout for help. I was just about to open my mouth to call someone when I heard Sara's voice.

"I wondered where you had got to, I was thinking you….. Oh, God, who's that? Are you ok?" She immediately crouched beside me. I quickly explained the situation, pleased I was no longer alone. "Right, Cam, call an ambulance now, explain exactly where we are. Then go and tell one of the security staff over by the entrance. They'll know what we need to do."

My phone lit up and I made a 999 call for the first time in my life. My hands were shaking and my voice was uneven as I explained what had happened. The call handler seemed calm and measured in her responses. She seemed to ask far too many questions. I just wanted someone to get an ambulance to us straight away. I looked down at Dr Smart, who now had Sara's jacket balled up under her head. There was a small string of saliva travelling down from the corner of her mouth.

"I'll stay with her, Cam, go and get security," said Sara softly. She was now sitting on the floor by Dr Smart, gently holding her hand and stroking her hair.

I pushed my way through the crowd of tipsy alumni, and spilled a few drinks on my way, not stopping to apologise. I found a security guard and explained what had happened. He made a quick call on his radio, and then gestured for me to show him where Dr Smart was. The crowd parted more easily for this tall, well-built gentleman than it had for me, although we did get a few curious glances.

The man introduced himself as Dan, and with a soft Newcastle accent explained to Dr Smart that we were going to move her into the recovery position. I instantly berated myself for not doing the same. He and Sara moved her with ease, and a woman emerged seemingly from nowhere with a pile of blankets. We tucked them around Dr Smart as best we could to protect her from the cold wind that was beginning to rise. Sara shivered, and was offered a blanket to replace the jacket that remained beneath Dr Smart's head. She politely declined. For a moment there was quiet as we all sat or stood, waiting for the paramedics to arrive. The sound of the Thames met our ears, and the chatter from inside was beginning to abate. I checked my watch – my colleagues would be ushering people out and ordering them cabs now.

The paramedics didn't take long, and part of me wondered whether the fact that this was the House of Lords had had an impact on that. A man and a woman in green jump suits immediately changed the feel of the terrace – from nervous waiting to calm action. They talked quietly to one another, and me, Sara and Dan moved away a little to make some room for them to work. I took that opportunity to pop my head round into the room. I met Tom's eyes and he came over.

"What's going on? I saw the paramedics? Everything ok?" he asked, his brow furrowing.

"It's Dr Smart. She's collapsed. She's unconscious."

"Oh God, ok, everyone's going now so there should be plenty of room to bring her through."

"Thanks, Tom." I felt my lower lip begin to wobble, wishing I had the same kind of fortitude that everyone else involved seemed to be displaying.

He spoke again. "Hey, darling, come and have a hug, you're doing grand. Are you going to come back with us?"

"No," I said into his aftershave soaked collar, "I need to stay with her. I'll leave the joys of the fun bus to you."

"Ok sweetie, I'll let Damien know. Where are you going to stay?"

"No idea, but to be honest that's not really a priority right now. Besides, Sara's here, I'm sure we can sort something out."

A worry line creased his forehead. "Be careful, Cam."

"I will." I turned back to the terrace to see the paramedics emerging into the room with Dr Smart on the stretcher. They cut through the remaining crowd swiftly, and Sara and I followed. I felt her steadying arm on my back as we made our way through a myriad of corridors that I didn't recognise. We emerged out into the dark night air in a small courtyard I hadn't been through when we arrived earlier in the evening. The ambulance was waiting quietly, blue lights flashing, bathing the courtyard in an eerie glow. The air seemed a little warmer here than it had by the water's edge. Dr Smart's face was still vacant, her eyes closed. The skin on her face seemed almost translucent in the emergency lighting. She was gently lifted into the back of the vehicle, and the doors were slammed shut. Sara took my hand, and showed me out onto the street. I suppose we must have gone through security somewhere along the way, but I don't remember it if we did. She stepped out into the road and hailed a black cab. Within minutes we were on our way to hospital behind the ambulance. It felt as though we travelled painfully slow, smells of petrol and sounds of frustrated car horns invading my anxieties. Sara held my hand.

"She's going to the best place, darling, they'll already be treating her in the ambulance, and they'll be ready for her in the emergency department." I nodded, not really able to say much that made any sense. My brain felt like it had melted into a leaden lump of fear, anxiety and tension.

After the frenetic activities of the past 30 minutes, the arrival at the hospital was something of a contrast. We were led to a waiting area where we sat, for over an hour, before anything happened at all. Somewhere else, I assumed, there was rapid, efficient medical activity. I hoped.

"Want a cuppa?" I asked, nodding at the vending machine in the airless room we sat in.

"It will be awful tasteless slop, but I suppose it is something to do, Cam. Are you ok?"

"Yeah. Tea withdrawal is hitting me hard though." I tried to smile, and headed to the machine with loose change. There was something utterly depressing about the cream coloured thin plastic cups that burned my fingertips as I brought them back over to the shiny fixed seats we had colonised. A man who looked as though he had been in a fight was lying across four of them nearby, snoring loudly.

I sat back down, and Sara put an arm around my shoulders. "You've done all you can, darling." She gently kissed my cheek, and squeezed my shoulder. The smell of her hair calmed me a little for a moment. There was a warmth I felt when I was with her that I hadn't experienced for far too long. "So do you do those posh drinks things often then?"

I laughed. "No, not really. I end up in all kinds of places – most often Starbucks and Costa. Occasionally I frequent the odd global company's glitzy canteen, and sometimes even a London hotel."

"Now that just sounds naughty!"

"Behave, Sara! It's mostly for a good steak and sparkling water, as I think you well know."

"We'll have to do something about that darling." Her eyes sparkled, and this time she leaned in to kiss me properly. I allowed my eyes to close, and my body moulded to hers. I took a deep breath in as I leaned away. "Stay at mine tonight, darling, I'm not letting you get a train tonight." I nodded, in no state to disagree. I hadn't even thought about how I would get home. I would surely have missed the 'fun bus' by now.

I took her free hand in mine. "Thank you so much, Sara, I don't know what I would have done without you tonight." I felt a tear drop down my cheek, and dropped my head.

"Rubbish, you'd have been fine. It's my pleasure to be here with you though. It's nice to be able to look after you a bit."

"Cameron Strawbank?" I looked up to see a male nurse calling my name. I stood and walked over, beckoning Sara to come with me. I found my hands fiddling with the buttons of my jacket. The nurse barely made eye contact, just confirming my name and that I came in with 'Mrs Smart'.

"Dr Smart," I corrected. "Yes, I brought her in."

"Are you family?"

"No, I'm a friend." The description wasn't completely accurate, but it seemed to be the simplest thing to say.

The nurse started walking, so Sara and I followed him, hoping this was the right thing to do. We were taken to a small cubicle surrounded by curtains. The nurse ushered us in.

"I'll let Mrs Smart explain," he said, leaving us. It was a huge relief to see Dr Smart conscious. She was propped up on pillows and looked somewhat pale, but I could see in her grey eyes she wasn't beaten.

"Has he gone?" She asked before we had a chance to say anything.

"Who?"

"That nurse. He's a bloody fool. Barely made eye contact with me. If he had been one of my nurses, I'd have given him some choice words, I can tell you." She spoke quietly and evenly. I laughed at the cross looking face, becoming aware of Sara.

"I think you met Sara earlier this evening?"

"No, I didn't actually, but a pleasure to meet you now – you're that MP aren't you? Well good for you, girl." Sara smiled graciously.

"I'm so pleased to see you looking a little better. Do they know what happened?" I took in the drip and the heart monitor she was hooked up to, and the hospital gown she was now wearing. I wondered what had happened to her elegant clothes.

"Minor stroke," she sniffed, reaching a shaky hand out for the glass of water by her side. "Had one before a few years back. Bloody annoying."

"Crikey, that sounds serious." I wasn't sure there was anything minor about a stroke.

"I'm old, Cameron. This is what happens to old people. But look," she took another sip, "no dribbling, no slurring of speech. I'm ok for now."

"Glad to hear it," I said, marvelling at the woman's nonchalance. "Is there anything we can get you?"

"No thanks. You've done more than enough. I gather it was you who raised the alarm."

"Well, yes, but thankfully there were others there – Sara for one." I looked gratefully at Sara's solemn face. "Can we contact anyone for you?"

"No thanks dear. I don't really have anyone who'd be interested. I have a great niece somewhere that I haven't seen in years, but this would only worry her. I'm fine." She folded her arms. The subject was closed.

The nurse came back in and without speaking started to take Dr Smart's blood pressure.

"Excuse me," said Dr Smart briskly, "you can come back and do that once my friends have gone. They shan't be here much longer."

"I need to..." started the nurse.

"You are here to take care of me young man. You can take my blood pressure in five minutes' time and no sooner." He opened his mouth to speak again, but thought better of it. He turned and walked out of the cubicle, tangling himself in the curtain as he left.

Sara jabbed me in the ribs, and I tried not to laugh. "Now then, you two," said the doctor who was once again in control. It was as though it were her hospital. "Do you have somewhere to stay? It's too late for you to be travelling home now."

Sara smiled. "It's taken care of," she said. "I have an apartment close by, and Cameron will stay there with me."

"Good, I always hoped you were a decent sort."

With that, it was clear it was time for us to go. We said our goodbyes, and left her bedside like dutiful schoolgirls.

"God, she's a force of nature," said Sara once we got into the back of a black cab.

"Isn't she?" I checked my watch. It was late. "I'm tired." My head was beginning to pound and the idea of a soft inviting bed felt like it might be a mirage. I had expended so much nervous energy this evening. Sara put her arm around me gently.

"I'm glad I'm taking you home. You need looking after. You're ever so pale. I think a hot drink and bed for you when we get in. I might even let you have a tot of brandy," said Sara. There was something reassuring about her confidence and care. It wasn't something I was used to.

"Do you think she'll be ok?"

"Do you think she'd allow them to make her anything other than ok?!" said Sara.

"Good point." Rush hour was long over, and we were back at Sara's in a very short time.

Chapter 9

For once Sara's apartment felt cold and dark. My legs were weak. "You look ready for bed, darling," said Sara, placing her hand gently on my shoulder. "Go and raid the top drawer in the unit by the bed for some pyjamas and make yourself comfy. I'll bring some hot chocolate through. I smiled gratefully, failing to find the energy to speak, and still slightly amazed that Sara Lorenzo was really mine.

I found a set of pale green cotton pyjamas with a button-up top. They fit well and soon I was tucked up chastely in the large bed in which we had rehearsed very different kinds of scenes in recent weeks. Within a few minutes, Sara came into the room, two mugs of steaming chocolate and a plate of buttery toast for us to share. She placed the tray gently on the bed and vanished into the en-suite. "No crumbs," she called over her shoulder, as I tucked into the toast. I hadn't realised I was so hungry until that moment. I cautiously sipped the scalding liquid, savouring the sweetness and darkness of chocolate melted in milk. It felt highly decadent.

"There better be some left for me," said Sara. She was freshly showered, her wet hair hanging on her shoulders. She had changed into some little shorts and a comfortable T-shirt that looked as though it had seen better days, but even so made me feel a little less chaste than I had just a moment before. There was something about the effortlessness of it that made her appeal to every cell in my being.

"You can have everything," I said, as if under a spell. Sara raised an eyebrow. "No, I mean it," I said, as she joined me in bed. "You can have all of me. You make me feel like a whole person, like I can be free and creative and alive, you care but you don't suffocate me." I held my hands up in front of my face as I continued. "I don't expect you to love me back, and that's not why I'm saying it, will say it. I just want you to know how I feel and the impact you've had on me. It's not cool, I'm not playing a game and I'm definitely not playing hard to get. I just love you." I picked up my mug once more and took a sip, having emptied the emotional payload that had been threatening to overflow for weeks. I breathed out slowly and then took another gulp.

Sara's face hadn't moved throughout the words I'd spoken, and for a moment she said nothing. She reached her hands out, and cupped my own, which still grasped the mug. "I'm going to make you hot chocolate in bed more often, Cam." She leaned forward and kissed me tenderly on the lips. "I love you too. Games are for players, and I am not one of those. I didn't expect this, I wasn't looking for this, but it is true. You are honest, passionate, sensitive and kind. I don't know what an old egotist like me did to deserve you." A single tear fell down my cheek, deflating the pressure that had built in my throat as she'd begun her little speech. For a while we simply sat quietly, contemplating the words we'd said, drinking from our cups and finishing the toast, which had now gone cold.

I fell asleep very soon after that, comforted by her hand stroking my hair gently in time to my lengthening breaths. As I dropped off, I couldn't believe I had ever been happier in my life.

The following morning, we left early – Sara to the Commons and me to the hospital. I walked onto the ward where I was informed Dr Smart was now recovering well. I overheard her harassing the nursing staff, instructing them she needed to be discharged as soon as possible. "And this weakness I'm feeling, I know it shouldn't keep me in hospital," she said firmly to the young nurse standing by her bed, looking like she'd rather be anywhere else, "but it might be sensible for you to summon a physiotherapist to give me some exercises to do so I can return to normal sooner rather than later." Dr Smart nodded, as if releasing the girl, who practically sprinted into another part of the ward.

"You sound like you're improving, Dr Smart," I said as I stood by her bed.

"Yes, thank you, just a minor annoyance really. Do sit down." She gestured towards the chair by the bed.

"Thank you. I'm glad things are working themselves out for you. You really scared me there."

"Oh don't worry, Ms Strawbank, I'm made of tough stuff. Your legacy will need to wait I'm afraid." I raised my eyebrows. "Just my little joke. I know that's not why you're here. I updated my will years ago, I just never told the college." I breathed again, relieved she didn't see me as a heartless blood sucker. "Who else would I leave my estate to?"

"Well, that's very generous of you."

"Oh rubbish, it's just sensible. I'm hoping that one day I'll be able to support others to enter the medical profession. Times may change, but there will always be a need for good doctors."

"Well I think everyone can agree with that."

"I'd say so. Especially your friend Ms Lorenzo." I tried to stop myself blushing. I failed. "I'm hearing disturbing rumours about the government bidding to charge for GP appointments. I think she'll give them a run for their money, don't you?"

"Oh yes, I think so. She's passionate about protecting the health service. And it will of course be a key General Election issue as and when it is finally called."

Dr Smart took a sip of water and nodded. "That said, I'm not sure about the leader of the opposition. He doesn't seem to have that much oomph about him does he?"

I laughed. "Ok, I'm convinced, you are definitely much recovered from last night."

Dr Smart smiled. "Of course. Now then, you must have things to attend to."

"Well, I do need to be getting back to Knighton for work. Just so long as you are ok though. Do you have everything you need?"

"Yes, thank you, I will be fine." She looked over to a nurse who appeared to be covertly checking her mobile phone. "You there, can you chase that physio up please?" The nurse looked up, shocked, nodded her head and vanished.

I happily made my way to the station, and caught the next train home, allowing the events of the last 24 hours to wash over me as the scenery sped past. When I arrived I went straight into the office hoping no one noticed my lateness. Tom was at his desk, looking a little pale, surrounded by empty coffee cups. "Heavy night on the fun bus?" Tom gave a sardonic laugh at my quip.

"Something like that. I ended up going for a quick drink when we got back with an old friend." He need say no more. By the look of him he'd only had a couple of hours sleep. I wondered whether this friend was a particularly 'friendly' friend. I resolved to get the gossip from him once his hangover had retreated.

Chapter 10

I was woken by the phone just after 6am. Confused and half asleep I fumbled for the handset. Damien. I furrowed my brow, anxiety bringing me fully awake. "Hi," I said, trying to sound like I hadn't just woken up. Which seemed a strange thing to do, as most people would still be asleep at this hour.

"What the hell is going on, Cameron?" His voice was panicky and loud.

"Sorry, Damien, I don't understand. What do you mean?"

"Bring up a news page now." I grabbed my tablet, and keyed in the name of a red top. The headline was unmistakable.

Donations for sex – shadow minister caught in lesbian tryst.

Below it was a granulated photo of me and Sara sitting side by side, her reaching a hand out to my cheek. For a moment I couldn't place the blurred snap. But it came back to me. The hospital.

"I, God, Damien, no, it's not like that." I whispered.

"So you're not shagging her then?" he demanded.

"No, it's not that. The two things are separate."

"You're telling me that she gives you ten grand and then you sleep with her, and it's not how it sounds? What kind of idiot are you?"

"Look, Damien, this is as much a shock to me as it is to..."

"I doubt that," he cut in. "I'm fairly sure you were aware you were sleeping with a shadow minister."

"I'm sorry Damien, look, can I come in and explain?" I ran my hand through tangled hair, not entirely confident I would be able to explain to his satisfaction.

"You'd better bloody had. I want you in my office by 7.30am." He hung up. I took several deep breaths and immediately thought of Sara. I selected her number and pressed 'call'.

Line busy.

I tried again.

Line busy.

I sent a text asking her to contact me urgently. Then, in desperation, I called Tom. He'd been asleep too. When I directed him to the page, he simply said one word. "Fuck." There was a long pause. There really was nothing I could add to that sentiment. "Shall I come over?"

"No, thanks, Tom, I've got to get showered and then go in to see Damien. Can we catch up later?"

"Sure. Shit. God, I'm sorry, Cam."

"It's not your fault, Tom, we knew this had the capacity to go wrong. I just don't know what I'm going to do to fix it. I just don't know where they got it from. How did they get it, Tom?"

"I don't know, darling, I don't know." He sighed heavily, and then swore liberally at the journalist who had claimed the exclusive. "I," he started to speak again and then paused. Then he coughed a couple of times. "Um, I have to go, hun. The doorbell just went."

"Sure, Tom, speak soon."

"Yeah," he said breathlessly. Then all was quiet. It was tempting to return to bed and go back to sleep, pretending none of this madness was happening. At the same time, I felt so wired I knew I wouldn't be able to sleep even if I tried. I made a beeline for the shower, and within half an hour I was in the car driving to the office. This was not going to be pretty.

I parked near a newsagent on campus, venturing in to see the story had made the front page. I picked up a copy, and gathered a packet of biscuits and some milk with it to try and camouflage it. I doubted the shopkeeper cared much about who I was, but I felt exposed. I checked my watch. I still had 15 minutes before I had to see Damien. I climbed back into the car, chucked the biscuits and milk onto the passenger seat, and took a deep breath. I closed my eyes, and slowly breathed out, in an effort to slow my racing heart rate.

My stomach turned as I read the opening lines of the article.

Shadow minister Sara Lorenzo has been caught exchanging sex for donations in a new scandal to hit her party just months before a likely General Election.

She is photographed here with an unnamed woman who, a source tells us, is the lesbian lover of Lorenzo, the MP for Mallington South. Sources have confirmed that the woman accepted £10,000 as a donation to Knighton University College's charitable fund in return for sex.

The photograph was taken by Philip Humphries who said: "They were clearly keen to be alone together when I saw them in the hospital waiting room. It was all kissing and cuddles, like there was no one else there. I was waiting to be seen, and couldn't help but notice."

You couldn't help but take a picture on your phone you nasty little man.

It is understood that the pair were waiting for news of a patient who has also made a donation to the University College. The involvement of Lorenzo with this woman, and the member of college staff has yet to be confirmed.

The college source, who cannot be named for legal reasons, mentioned the woman in hospital, saying: "If the college plays its cards right she'll probably leave a legacy in her will."

I gasped. Not only was I being framed as some kind of charitable hooker, it appeared I was leaning over an elderly woman rubbing my hands in glee as she teetered between life and death. I put my head in my hands. This was getting worse. I rubbed my eyes, before folding the paper inwards on itself. I didn't need to read any more. Damien was waiting for me, and I had very few options.

I stood up straight, and walked as confidently as I could manage, into the building. I switched my phone to silent. The building was quiet, with just the sounds of a hoover coming from down a corridor. I walked to Damien's office and knocked. There was a brief pause, before I heard his voice call.

Damien's face was red, and his hands were clasped together from where he sat behind his desk. He didn't invite me to sit, so I remained standing. Somehow I felt better that way. "You really need to explain yourself, Cameron."

"It's not about sex Damien. It's not, I swear. We're in a relationship."

"Were you in one before she wrote you that cheque?" He asked, pointedly.

"No. Well, not really." It was complicated. How to explain the start of something so accidental?

"What does that mean? Let me ask you more baldly. Did you sleep with her before or after she gave you £10,000?"

I swallowed before I spoke. "Before. And she gave the college £10,000 not me."

"In return for your services?"

"No."

"So it was unrelated?"

"Yes."

"But you met her because she was your prospect."

Pause.

"Yes." I wanted to run out of the room, out of the building, off campus and away to somewhere before this awful morning had begun so harshly.

"I think you need to..."

"I'll save you the breath Damien. I resign. I assume you won't want me to serve my notice." He seemed surprised, but his face gave away his relief.

"No. I think that is appropriate. We will pay you to the end of your notice period." I nodded my thanks, and started to leave the room. "I'll have someone from the press office call you." I opened the door, and practically sprinted to my car, desperately trying to hold back the tears.

Once in the car, I could hold on no longer. I sat, head on the steering wheel, and sobbed. I don't know how long I was there for. After what could have been five minutes, or an hour, I attempted to wipe my face with the sole tissue I found in the glove compartment. I picked up my phone. I had nine missed calls. I couldn't face them now. I put the phone back in my pocket, and put the key in the ignition. Home was the only place I could bear to be now.

I walked through my front door, locked it and put the chain on. I sat on the sofa and once more looked at my phone. Another two missed calls. Four were from Sara, two were from a college number and five were from withheld numbers. There were several voicemails, but before I listened to anything, I needed to speak to Sara. The guilt of placing her on the front page of the tabloids weighed me down like lead. Her number rang. And rang. No answer. Finally it went through to voicemail. I didn't know what to say beyond: "Sara, it's Cam. Call me."

I started to work through my voicemails. One was from the college press officer, who wanted to speak to me later on in the morning when I had a chance. The next was from HR, letting me know I needed to confirm my resignation in writing as soon as possible. The next was from Sara.

"Hi. By now you'll have seen the papers. God, this is a nightmare. Look, I need to get to a meeting now at Millbank. I won't be reachable. Don't do anything, don't speak to anyone. I'll call you." There was something oddly dispassionate and remote about her voice. I went cold. I had just lost my job. I hadn't considered I might lose Sara as well.

The next voicemail was from a reporter. "Cameron Strawbank. We have a source that confirms that you are the woman in today's donations for sex story. We want to give you the chance to tell your side of this story. My name is Richard Lenton. Call me on..."

I replayed the message, and wrote down the number before pressing save. I went to the kitchen to make myself a cup of tea. I returned and dialled.

"Yes, it's Cameron Strawbank. I think we need to talk." The voice on the other end of the phone confirmed he would come to meet me at home in the next hour. I sighed, and tried Tom's number again. His line was busy.

There was nothing left to do. I wrote a brief resignation letter and emailed it to HR. I looked at the clock. It was 9.45am. I felt like my rude awakening was days ago. I felt tired. All the feelings of anger, anxiety, injustice, fear and indecision had taken their toll. I was drained. I curled up on the sofa and drifted into a fitful sleep.

Chapter 11

The doorbell went an hour and a half later. My head hurt and my eyes were sore. I glanced at the mirror as I picked myself up off the sofa. I looked like I hadn't slept for a week. I quickly tried to make my hair look less like it had been slept on as I walked towards the front door nervously. I unlocked it, and pulled, but it abruptly stopped short. I'd forgotten the chain. I shut the door again, squeaking an apology at the young man whose ear I glimpsed briefly. I released the chain and then reopened the door.

"Hi, come in." He was a portly chap, with a burgundy coloured v neck jumper over a light blue shirt open at the collar.

"Thank you. I'm Simon, I'm from the press office. We spoke earlier." He paused and sat where I pointed. "And for the record, don't just invite a random stranger into your home again before checking exactly who they are. Make sure you ask for ID." He sighed, his balding head red and shiny under my kitchen lights. "Sorry to be so autocratic, I just need to make sure you know the situation you're in." I smiled, unsure of what to say. It was good to have someone to talk to.

"Do you want a cuppa?"

"Thanks," he said, taking a hanky from his pocket and wiping his brow. "Do you have any biscuits? It's been a long morning."

I laughed quietly. "I know."

"Yes, sorry, Cameron, it's no doubt been a tough one for you as well."

We sat together at my small kitchen table together and Simon began to speak. "Ok, so technically I'm here to protect the reputation of the college. However, think of me as someone who can lend you a bit of a hand too."

I breathed a small sigh of relief. I was glad I wasn't alone, and I was pleased I had called the college press office.

"Technically, in a few weeks you will no longer be an employee, so the college could hang you out to dry," he said, dunking a rich tea biscuit into his well sugared tea. "But in all honesty, it's not a great tactic, as long as you play it right. My advice to you? Say nothing."

"You're the second person to say that to me today."

"Sara?" I nodded. "Ok, so for now they don't have your name but in truth, it's only a matter of time."

"I've already had a call from Richard Lenton." Simon frowned, putting his biscuit down for a moment.

"Have you spoken to him?"

"No, that's why I called you."

"Good. We're going to put out a statement later on. We won't confirm your identity, and unless you confirm it yourself, it will be harder for them to name you." He drained his cup, seemingly oblivious to the scalding temperature the tea must still be at. "May I?" he asked, looking at the plate.

"Sure, I've lost my appetite," I said. My head swam. The remark he made as he walked through my front door about asking for ID and being careful who I let in began to make more sense. "Excuse me, I need to use the bathroom."

I looked at my face in the mirror. The one that had appeared on the front page of one of the country's biggest selling newspapers. My thoughts turned again to Sara. I felt sick. I knelt by the toilet, and my half cup of tea came back up into the bowl. I washed my face, and resolved to get my conversation with Simon over with.

"Here's my number," he said, handing over a dog-eared business card. "Are you ok?"

"No, not really."

"Have you heard from Sara?" he asked. I hardened my eyes and looked at him, but his face was sympathetic.

"Not properly. I think she's got quite a lot going on at her end. I'm hoping to speak to her later on."

"Good. Ok. You need to be careful though. Do you have people here? People who you can rely on I mean?"

I thought immediately of Tom. "Yes, I do."

"Make sure you look them up. This stuff is tough." I felt my lower lip begin to wobble. "Here." He took the business card that had been sitting on the table back. He scribbled something on it and handed it back. "If you need anything, call me on this. It's my home number."

I smiled and thanked him politely.

He didn't stay much longer and as he left I thanked him for his time, and locked and chained the door after him.

I tried Sara's phone again. The line was busy again. I wondered who she was talking to rather than me. Acid rose up my gullet, and I fought the urge to be sick again. I sat back down at the kitchen table and opened my diary. I was teased by Tom for still carrying a paper one. But I liked the realness of a schedule I could get to grips with physically. Today I cursed it. An electronic calendar could be reset to automatically delete appointments associated with a particular organisation. A paper one could not. I reached for a blue biro and started to neatly cross out the meetings one by one in my diary for the following week. There were many more in there, but they could wait until I could face them. The now empty week stretched out in front of me. Frustrated tears fell onto the page one by one.

"Cam, sorry, it's been an awful morning." said Sara

"I know," I said as I answered the call that Sara had finally made a few hours later.

"I got hauled into HQ first thing and I've been with the media team ever since."

"Are you ok?" I asked.

"Yes, but I'm not sure I'm going to keep my cabinet seat." There was something perfunctory about the conversation we were having.

"I'm so sorry, Sara, this is all my fault." My voice caught and faltered.

"It's not your fault, Cam, it's not. It's just a really bad situation. We're both in it."

I sighed. "Yes, that is true, I can confirm."

"Well at least you haven't been named." I could hear Sara hailing a cab in the background of the call, and wondered where she was going now.

"I may as well have been. I've lost my job and reporters have begun calling me." There was a pause on the line.

"Hell, sorry, darling, that's awful. God I'm sorry. What happened?"

"I resigned."

"No, I mean with the reporters."

"I haven't said anything." I felt anxiety surge again into my stomach.

"Good." she sounded relieved. "So why did you quit?"

"I jumped before they could sack me."

"What did you do that for? They can't just sack you like that, they need to hear your side."

"You read the piece, Sara. It was pretty obvious I couldn't go back. I had no choice. It was made really clear to me." I stood up and walked to the cool tiles on the kitchen wall and rested my forehead on them. "I really wish you were here."

There was a pause. "You know I can't. There are photographers following my every move, wanting to follow me to you. It wouldn't help." I stifled my tears.

"I love you, Sara. You know that right?"

"I know, darling, I know. I love you too, Cam. But we have to hang on for a bit."

I stood up straight for a moment.

"What do you mean?"

"I mean we need to stay apart for a while. We can't carry on like this knowing what will happen."

"But they'll stop eventually, surely?"

"Only if we're careful, Cam. Listen, I've taken advice. I know it's bad but there's nothing else we can do."

I tried to swallow the sobs which threatened to overwhelm me. "Ok. How long, a few days?"

"Darling, look, they might even have bugged our phones. This is going to take longer than a day or two to cool off. I'm so sorry. There's nothing I can do."

"Nothing you can do," I repeated. "So that's it."

"No, Cam, no. Just for a while."

"How long's a while, Sara? Until next month? Until the election? When?" My voice rose, and there was no mistaking my upset now.

"Look, I'm sorry. I'm sorry. It's such a mess. But it's not forever."

"It may as well be." I was aware I was sounding like a petulant child, but I couldn't help myself. "I can see where your priorities lie. You said you loved me. It didn't mean anything did it?"

"Oh God, Cam, yes, of course it did." She took a deep breath. "For the first time, in so long. I don't want this to be over, I don't."

"But your career comes first," I said resignedly.

"No, that's not what I'm saying."

"Then what?"

"God I hate doing this stuff over the phone."

"Then let me see you. I'll come to London, I'll find a hotel somewhere we can meet in secret. Anything. Let's work things out."

"No, Cam. No, we can't. It would be foolhardy." There was a silence. "Please don't make me choose, Cam. We can get through this."

"I don't think we can right now. I haven't made you choose. You have simply made your choice haven't you?"

"No, Cameron, please, don't let this happen, I know you, this isn't what you want. Talk to me."

"I don't have anything else to say."

"Right," came Sara's voice, sounding defeated. "I'll go."

"Bye," I whispered.

"Bye." The phone went dead. I sank down the kitchen wall to sit on the floor. I buried my head in my hands, dropping the phone on the floor. It was ringing again. Tom. I couldn't bring myself to answer. I had nothing to say, let alone any ability to say it.

Chapter 12

A few hours later, exhausted and dehydrated with tears, I looked at my phone once more to find a text from Tom, saying he was going to come over after work. I poured a large glass of water, gulped some painkillers for my pounding head, and made my way into the living room. I turned some mindless television on. I heard a sound outside, and peered through the front window, hoping Tom had managed to make it out of work early. I could do with a friendly face. I saw a black four-wheel drive, out of which a camera lens poked. I was too slow to move quickly enough, and saw a flash emanate from the vehicle. I swiftly drew the curtains, but not before I saw someone else dart out of the car and make her way towards the front door, notepad clutched in hand. The doorbell went soon after. Instinctively I switched off the TV and turned off the lights, as though it would make the journalist think I wasn't in, in spite of her having seen me for herself. My breathing began to calm and I went into my bedroom. I climbed into bed and texted Tom, telling him not to come over. The last thing I wanted was for him to get dragged into this. I sighed. He had told me to be careful and now look at me. The doorbell went once again. I pulled the duvet over my head and closed my eyes.

It was dark by the time I woke up. I cautiously peered out of the window. The car was gone, and I couldn't see anyone. Relieved, I looked at my watch. It was after 9pm. I thought about ordering some food for delivery, but somehow even that felt risky at the moment. I checked my phone, half expecting a message from Sara. There was none. There was a text from Tom, thanking me for tipping him off. He'd had to go up north at the last minute for work on the 8pm train, so I wouldn't see him for a few days anyway. Another message from Richard Lenton. I deleted it before it completed. What exactly was my side of the story even if I was going to give it? While the papers were wrong about mine and Sara's motives, everything else was factually accurate. My side of the story would sound like semantics. All over again the injustice of the situation hit me.

I threw together a quick meal of beans on toast and opened a bottle of red wine. I wasn't usually a lone drinker but tonight felt like an appropriate exception. I felt like the only person alive.

It was while I was washing up, being comforted by its normality that there was a gentle tap on the door. I jumped, having assumed that the press would have left for their own homes by now. I contemplated ignoring it, but the fact that whoever it was hadn't used the doorbell intrigued me. It might not be a reporter. My hopes rose and I ventured towards the door. I put my hands against the wood and tentatively spoke. "Who is it?"

"It's me," my heart sank. It wasn't Sara and I struggled to immediately place the muffled voice. "Hayley." My eyebrows rose in surprise. I was not expecting her. Instinctively I undid the chain, unlocked and opened the door, to find her with a carrier bag from the local supermarket in one hand and a bottle of red in the other. She smiled and walked in. I closed the door behind her, pleased to see a familiar face after such an odd day. "I saw the papers, and when I drove past after work I could see a photographer lurking. I'm figuring your lady love won't be coming anywhere near, so I figured you'd need this," she proffered the bottle, "and this." She opened the carrier bag to enable me to see the enclosed chocolate, crisps and popcorn.

"Thanks." She was the first person without an agenda who I'd spoken to all day.

"Did you say anything to them?" She jerked her thumb towards the window. I shook my head. "Want to talk about it?" I thought for a moment.

"Not much. I lost my job today. And my girlfriend and I am front page tabloid fodder. There is nothing much else to say." I gave a laugh that I couldn't even pretend related to genuine humour. Hayley topped up my wine and poured herself a liberal glass.

"Well frankly, that all sounds like a pile of poo. I suggest we watch a dreadful action movie, drink wine and eat crap for the rest of the evening." I smiled.

"Deal."

It was the early hours before I went to bed. Hayley had had too much wine to drive home and slept on the sofa. I was woken at 9am the following morning with a hot cup of tea. Hayley was already showered and dressed. "God, I can't believe I've slept this late."

"You needed it sweetie," said Hayley, hopping onto the bed next to me with her own half-drunk mug of tea. "I have no idea how you have been coping, holed up in this little place for the last 24 hours while that circus was going on."

"Well maybe it will die down now," I said, sitting up slowly.

"Sorry, babe, I wouldn't count on it." She passed me her tablet.

The headline screamed from the screen:

Embattled MP apologises for lapse in judgement.

Reading on, the statement was printed in full, along with a picture of Sara, which looked as though it had been snatched as she hurried from a car to a meeting. She looked pale and drawn and her eyes were dark.

Sara Lorenzo said: "It was a grave error in judgement which represents a moment of foolishness rather than a genuine attempt at corruption. I want to offer my apologies to my constituents and the party, and I have plans to put this episode behind me."

The article went on to say that she had offered her resignation to the party leader, who had refused to accept it.

"A moment of foolishness," I said under my breath.

"I'm so sorry, Cam, you really deserve better," said Hayley gently, putting an arm around me.

"I really do." I sniffed, and laughed and then sobbed. The situation seemed almost comical. I scanned the rest of the article. Still no mention of my name, but there was a statement from the College.

"Our work, providing additional support to valuable areas of the college, continues to be of great importance. While we cannot comment on the detail of this recent allegation, we can confirm that yesterday a member of the development team chose to hand in their resignation with immediate effect. In the light of recent events, we will be reviewing our ethics policy and procedures, as well as providing enhanced screening as part of staff recruitment."

I turned my head to the ceiling. "They said they wouldn't hang me out to dry."

"Babe, they haven't. They haven't named you."

"Yeah, but everyone there will know exactly who I am and why I've gone. It's a small industry. I'll never get another major gifts job in the UK again."

"Come here, Cam, forget it for now. You've got three months' pay, a broken heart and no work to do. Honestly? I think you should run away to a desert island for the next six weeks." I allowed Hayley to take me into her arms, grateful for her familiar scent. I couldn't imagine leaving the flat, let alone the country, but the image was a sweet one. "Who in God's name let this out anyway?"

"I don't know, I really don't." I looked at my phone, but there was still nothing from Sara. "Not that it really matters now. I think I have been most conclusively ex-communicated by both Sara and the college."

"Yeah well, no points for guessing where her priorities lie. Her career is the be all and end all right?"

"Well yes, but I guess that's to be expected. I don't know why I expected anything different really. She has done what she has to do to keep her job."

"While you're here having lost yours, with a broken heart to boot. Charming."

"I'm sure she'd contact me if she could," I said, hoping it was true. Hayley gave a rueful smile. I suspected she was biting her tongue for my benefit.

"Is she really all that?" I looked at her for a moment, and once again dissolved into tears. My phone began to ring – it was Tom. I reached for the almost empty box of tissues to try and quell the emotional flood before answering. I blew my nose and then picked up the call.

"Hi," I said. It came out as a croak.

"Hey, darling, I'm so sorry, how are you?"

"I've been better, I think that's safe to say."

"Have you heard from her today?"

"No. I doubt I will. She's got to save her career." There was a long pause. I could hear nervous breathing on the other end of the line.

"Look, Cam, I need to tell you something." I raised my eyebrows, curious as to what more I could possibly need to know. "I've found out who leaked the story to the press."

"Ok, you've got my attention." I put the phone onto loud speaker so Hayley could hear what Tom had to say.

"It was me. I mean, I didn't mean to, I didn't even know I was doing it. God I'm so sorry, I've wrecked everything."

I went cold. "What do you mean Tom? When did you speak to a journalist? I don't get it." Hayley's eyes were wide, and I could see anger building behind them.

"The drink I went for after the House of Lords event, with my old friend Rick. I had too much to drink and talked more than I should have. It had been a long night and I told him all that had happened and about you and Sara. It's all a bit hazy to be honest, but it wasn't until yesterday when I saw who the story was by that I realised what I'd done. Rick is Richard Lenton. I knew he worked in the media, but I didn't realise where." He stopped. I had no words of comfort to offer him.

"You were the one telling me to be careful. You said that it would all be fine." I took a deep breath. "I trusted you."

"I know Cam, I know. I was stupid and drunk and thought it was an amusing story to tell."

"Well great, I'm glad I was able to give you and your friend a laugh."

"No, darling, it wasn't like that. Please, I'm sorry, I really am. What can I do to make this better?"

"Nothing. I think you need to go now."

"But are you ok? Are you on your own? I don't want you to deal with this alone."

"I'm not alone, Tom. You and Sara aren't the only people in my life."

"Right, yes, of course. Ok, so, I'll go."

"Good bye." I pressed cancel gently.

"Cam?" Hayley's voice was quiet, but urgent. There was nothing I could say now. I was out of tears and inspiration. I put my head in my hands. I felt her come and perch next to me on the bed. I didn't move. I was glad she was near, but I wasn't sure there was anything she could do. A Facebook notification beeped on my mobile that was still beside me. Without looking at the screen I picked up the phone and threw it across the room. I looked up in shock when I heard it hit the wall in front of me with a terminal crunch. No good news had come from that device in days. I was better off without it. I stared at the white wall it had hit. There was a small grey scuff left behind. Hayley didn't say anything for a few moments. One thing I always appreciated about her was her ability to know when to stay quiet. After a few minutes, she got up, and I heard the kettle go on. My first cup of tea wasn't yet finished, but the idea of the follow up was a good one. If it had been later in the day and we were in a bar, she would have lined up a shot of something almost illegally strong for me. There was something comforting in that.

Chapter 13

24 hours later I was in the bar at the airport sipping a glass of European lager. "There's something about leaving the country that makes drinking before noon obligatory," said Hayley, already well into her first pint. I smiled broadly. I wasn't happy, but a kind of reckless abandon had taken me over in the last hour. It had happened the moment we checked in our baggage and walked through security. While we were still in the UK, we were now 'air-side', which represented escape. No phone to disturb me, and travelling to a country where no one knew me. This was a chance to take back some control.

"Thank you, Hayley," I said. "I don't know how you managed to sort this out, but thank you. Things were all getting a bit crazy."

"You're welcome. I was due some leave, and the air miles were just sitting there gathering dust…" she trailed off. Jet setting was part of her role as a sales rep for an international outdoor clothing company, as she described it to me. Air miles and expensive waterproofs were the perks of the job. "Besides, you need a friend right now, what with Tom and Sara and everything." I frowned, not wanting my thoughts to return to them yet again. Somehow, in the space of just 48 hours I had lost my job, my girlfriend and my best friend. "Another?" She pointed to my half empty glass.

"Yeah, why not?"

"That's my girl," she winked and went back to the bar. There was something about her. There always had been. There was a lot about herself that she held back, but I always remembered the time I ended up in hospital with food poisoning, it was her who, in spite of her inability to commit, had stayed by my bedside for 48 hours. There was a quiet voice in my head asking if it was wise to fly to the Balearic Islands with my ex-girlfriend. But right now, I planned to drown that voice with lager. And possibly something stronger later on.

Take-off, which usually made me nauseous, was exhilarating. I'm not sure if it was the alcohol, the company or the situation, but as the wheels left the tarmac, I felt a weight lift from my shoulders. I put headphones in and listened to an old but much loved album, losing myself in the thrill of running away and the fuzzy edges provided by earlier lubrication.

I looked beside me to see Hayley already dozing, her head slightly to one side. A seasoned flyer, she had mastered the art of getting sleep where she could. I wasn't sure how her long slender limbs had fitted so comfortably, but she certainly looked at home. I watched her breathe, and thanked her silently for being there when there was no one else. Her in-the-moment hedonism had been the end of our romantic involvement a year ago, but now it was just that which made her perfect. I didn't want anyone who was going to try and project any kind of future for me. I wanted someone to be with me here and now, who didn't want anything from me, and was prepared to enjoy each day as it came. It was as though I had fallen from the top of a skyscraper, and while I was falling she had casually spread out a net to break my fall.

I closed my eyes, in an effort to emulate my companion.

I felt a hand gently stroking my own and woke with a start. My eyes sprang open and I switched off the music. "How loud was that on?" asked Hayley, smiling, her hand still resting on mine. "We've just landed. We'll be off in a tick. I've organised a transfer, so we shouldn't need to hang around at the airport for long." I was still half asleep and nodded in agreement. "You're cute when you're sleepy." I blushed and looked away. She'd said that to me before.

"So what's the temperature like here then?" I smoothed down my clothes and undid my seatbelt, allowing Hayley's hand to drop.

"About 27 degrees according to the captain."

"Perfect."

"I'd like it a touch hotter, but I guess it will do."

"Such a sun worshipper," I teased. Hayley's colouring was unusual. While she had naturally blonde hair, she had dark skin that tanned easily. She jabbed me in the ribs, before levering herself up and reaching for her hand luggage.

The dry heat hit me as soon as I stepped out of the aeroplane, my jeans suddenly feeling unnecessarily thick and my jacket superfluous. It was a glorious sensation, feeling the warmth of the sun on my skin. Before long we were sitting in the large outdoor hotel bar, gazing across turquoise sea to the cliffs and trees across the bay we were staying in. We had done a swift change and were now both wearing far fewer clothes. I couldn't help but take in Hayley's collarbone, making the simple black vest top she wore seem so elegant. I closed my eyes to shake the image of what Sara might look like in the same position. Hayley took out a packet of cigarettes and put one in her mouth, lighting it with a sigh.

"God, you don't still smoke do you?"

"Of course. Why wouldn't I?" she said, out of the corner of her mouth, breathing smoke as she did so.

"Well, with the smoking ban and everything, so many people have gone over to e-cigarettes."

"Vaping shows a deep lack of commitment. Either smoke or don't, none of this pretend smoking crap. This, my dear, is a civilised country where you can smoke wherever you like."

A waiter appeared with two mojitos.

"Here's to a lovely holiday, fag ash Lil."

"Cheers!" Our glasses clinked and we both took healthy swigs of the drinks which seemed significantly stronger than those we were used to.

"Smoking and hard liquor, I feel bad behaviour is de rigueur in Ibiza."

"You said it, sister," said Hayley with a smile.

"I've never done a moonlight flit before. God knows what everyone will think. I just emailed my parents and told them not to worry and that I was going on holiday for a bit. I've not said anything to anyone else."

"Sod 'em. You're free. Enjoy it, honey." Hayley put her shades on, that owed something to Jackie Onassis, looking every bit the matinee idol as she gesticulated with her cigarette in one hand, and a cocktail umbrella in the other.

"Yes. I will. Thank you, Hayley, I don't know what I'd have done without you."

"Shut up, darling, you've already said that. God, you know me, any excuse for a drink and a holiday. You're doing me a favour. You deserve a break from all that crap. I'm just sorry I can only stay for a week."

"Yes, about that, why didn't you book my return flight for the same time as yours?"

"What have you got to go back to? You haven't got a job, no wife or kids. Enjoy it. Just book a flight when you're ready to come home – the air miles are there whenever you want them, Cam." I smiled, but wasn't sure what being here alone would be like. Determined to stay in the moment though, I pointed out a swanky looking yacht sailing across the bay.

"I wonder who that belongs to?"

"Ooh, a playboy millionaire and his mistress no doubt..."

"It's not all about sex you know."

"More's the pity." I gave Hayley a look of faux disapproval.

I felt comfortably inebriated as we started on our third mojito. It was late afternoon and the days spread out before us like a blanket. We watched other holiday makers come and go, observed the looks that went between various staff. We made up stories for each of them, laughing together as they became more and more outlandish. It was good to laugh, it felt therapeutic, as though I was letting something go. I laughed at myself, imagining emulating Elsa from Frozen, casting pillars of ice and swishing my hair. Let it go. Yes, that's what I should do. If all the events back home were in a box labelled 'England', I put a firm lid on it. Deep down I knew it wasn't going to go away, but at least perhaps I could place it on a high shelf out of reach for a time.

We returned to our room before dinner. I was in need of a shower. "Sorry about the double bed, it was a last minute booking, and this was the last room they had available," said Hayley.

I smiled, awkwardly. "Ah, it's fine. It's not like we've not shared before. I'm sure we'll cope."

Hayley bobbed her head and turned to the mirror beside the bed, brushing her hair that had become a little windswept thanks to the sea breeze.

I stepped into the shower and let the hot water envelop me. I felt tired, but in a comfortable way. The steam filled the large cubicle and my lungs. I breathed it in, feeling it cleanse me. I washed the rest of the UK from my skin and emerged into a soft white towel. Once dressed in dark blue jeans and a burgundy short sleeved shirt, I emerged, rejuvenated and ready for food.

"Come on then, Cam, let's eat. You'll thank me for booking us 'all inclusive' when you see the selection on offer – I saw them setting up as we walked back from the bar."

"Sounds good to me, although before I eat anything I need a nice cold drink of water."

"Lightweight."

"Oh be quiet, just because you can sustain yourself solely on spirits and cigarettes…" We emerged into the dining room. "Wow, you weren't wrong about the spread. That's pretty impressive. What is that melon supposed to be?"

"It's been carved into an octopus, see? It's a local speciality; there'll be something different every night," said Hayley glancing around the room for a table.

The meal passed mostly in companionable silence. I felt tired, and Hayley seemed happy to quietly eat and survey her surroundings. Every now and again I would catch her brow furrow, but only for a moment. I wondered what she had been doing for the past few months, whether there really was anyone special in her life. She'd always been pretty quiet about her emotions, and I'd never met her family. In truth, I knew very little about her. For all I knew, she had a girlfriend or boyfriend back home. That was how she was.

Initially when we were first together, she appeared to have no baggage, like the perfect girlfriend. There was no drama, no ex-partner, no unfinished business. Now I wondered if rather than having no baggage, she simply kept it below deck.

I refused the coffee that was offered. I could feel my body preparing for sleep, and I was happy to oblige. "Listen, Hayley, I'm going to head to bed. It's been a long few days and I really need to sleep. No, you stay, enjoy your coffee. I'll be fine." She smiled, and wished me goodnight as I stood. I walked away, past the chattering diners.

It was nice to vanish into the relative silence of our room. The only sound was the hum of the air conditioning. I walked over to the sliding door that opened out onto a small balcony with a sea view. I leaned on the balcony edge and gazed across the bay, watching boats slowly returning to their moorings, and people making their way to or from dinner. There was a gentle lapping sound from the sparkling azure sea a few floors below. Idyllic. I left the door open, walked back into the room and turned off the air conditioning. Once in thin cotton pyjamas, I climbed into the cool sheets. I felt anaesthetised by the alcohol, and the feeling of my head sinking into the fresh pillow was delicious. My mind swirled in a melee of sun, sea, melons and octopuses and I drifted pleasantly.

Chapter 14

I opened my eyes the following morning to sun streaming through a crack in the thick curtains. I had a sleepy recollection of a body joining me in bed some hours before. I was more asleep than awake when warm limbs and torso spooned me. I looked over at the other side of the bed. Hayley was facing away from me now, breathing peacefully. I wondered when she had moved, how long we had been close. I felt like I should analyse what that might be about, or double check whether it had simply been a vivid dream. But with the fingers of sleep still in my head, and the sun in my eyes, I forgot the analysis and sat up slowly. A bar of sunlight warmed my bare arm. I sleepily padded towards the balcony and slipped through the curtains. The world was new again. Boats were beginning to traverse the bay once more, and one or two people could be seen walking towards the small town that serviced the various hotels and villas nearby.

Two small wicker chairs were there beside a table, and I sat down. I had bare feet, but the smooth concrete balcony floor was warm from the sun. It was glorious. I leant back and closed my eyes. Unbidden, the memory of Hayley's arms around my shoulders from my sleepy memory drifted into my consciousness. They swiftly became Sara's arms, and face and voice and the words she had spoken to me. The gentle meaningless utterances of the mornings we had shared together. "Trust you to be sat out in the sun covered from head to toe in your dad's pyjamas," came a teasing voice from above me. I opened my eyes to see Hayley standing, hands on hips, wearing the cotton shorts and simple vest top she had slept in.

"Oi, these are mine. I can't see my dad wearing pale blue gingham, can you?" Hayley laughed.

"Well, perhaps not. They suit you though."

"Thanks. So do yours." I clasped my hands together. Suddenly uncomfortable, feeling awkward and lame complimenting her pyjamas. I looked out to sea trying to think of something else to say.

"Beautiful view isn't it? You should have seen the sunset last night. I sat and watched it from here. The sky was a gorgeous orange and purple. Stunning," said Hayley.

"Oh I know, totally gorgeous. You chose well."

"Thank you."

"I hope the breakfast is good, I'm starving."

The spread in the dining area put my usual cornflakes and builder's tea to shame. There was everything from fresh fruit, to cuts of meat and cheese, freshly made omelettes and pancakes and gallons of strong coffee. When I saw that I immediately thought of Sara. She would love this; the extravagance, the choice, the coffee. My stomach lurched. "You ok, babe?" asked Hayley, registering that I had glazed over.

"Yeah, sorry, just a bit overwhelmed by the choice. I feel it would be rude not to have a go at those lovely looking pancakes there. Look, that chap in the white hat makes them to order."

"Good call. Have you seen the selection of sauces, fruit and flavours there are to add to them?"

"I think breakfast may last a while," I said, firmly putting Sara back in the box marked 'England'.

We sat and ate for over an hour, admiring the view, looking at a map of the island, and beginning to make tentative plans. One thing was for sure though; this day was going to be a beach day. My body was still adjusting to the journey the day before, and a day lazing on a sun lounger with a book sounded like the best possible option.

"Well," said Hayley, wiping her mouth with her napkin, "I'm going to put my bikini on." She said it with a sparkle in her eye that did something unexpected to my pulse.

"Sounds like a plan," I said, attempting not to twinkle back at her, but failing.

"That's my girl," she said, squeezing my arm as we walked out of the dining room. My skin burned, erasing all thoughts of Sara. I was left with a feeling that was somewhere between guilt and desire. I trailed back to our room in her wake, glad she couldn't see the colour that had come to my cheeks.

In the hurry to leave the country I didn't even have any books with me, so I lay on my sun lounger, taking in the sea, the sky and the heat. There was something purifying about it. The sun was burning away the pain and the regret. I allowed myself to wonder what Sara was doing. All I could conjure up in my mind were the damp, grey streets of London, and her profile walking away from me down a street. I felt a dull ache as the vision faded.

"Cocktail?" asked Hayley.

"It's not even 10.30! No, not for me. I'll have another coffee though if you're heading in."

"Heading in? Not here Cam. Look." She gestured to one of the waiting staff, who came and took our order.

"I feel faintly uncomfortable letting someone else do my bidding like that."

"Ha! You didn't mind when it was me you were asking did you?"

"Naturally."

Over sips of drinks we commented on the view, made small talk, and enjoyed the surroundings.

"So, what do you think of him?" Hayley asked, pointing out a smart looking young man, wearing expensive looking loafers and short chinos. "Gay or European?"

I mulled it over. "Good question. The hair suggests gay, but the shoes suggest perhaps Italian."

"Good call. Let's opt for European," said Hayley, twirling her cocktail umbrella.

"Now of course, he could be both gay and European. They aren't mutually exclusive you know."

"Ever the diplomat. Of course, there's only one way of finding out."

"No, please, Hayley, let's leave the poor guy alone."

"I'm just being friendly." She drained her glass, stood up and followed Mr Loafer to the bar. She gave him the full routine – hair flick, looking at him from lowered lids, laughing loudly at what I assumed must be a joke he'd made. She walked back towards me with a swagger. "Camp as Christmas, French."

"Two out of two then."

"Nope. He has an unexpected wife." As if on cue, a tall, slim blonde walked up to Mr Loafer and planted a wet kiss on his lips. "Honeymoon."

"Well there you go. See, it's a ridiculous game." I said, pretending not to be amused.

"Rubbish, Cam, you love it. We'd have missed out on the drama of Jean – that's his name – had we not played."

"And this is why you are the perfect person to be with right now, Hayley. It's never serious with you, just fun and laughs. Thank you."

"Always?" Hayley smiled, popping her large shades down over her eyes. "I think I'll go and see if I can find a bonk-buster in the little shop by reception." She put down her cocktail and vanished into the hotel. I felt oddly deflated. I also felt a pang of guilt. Running off to the Mediterranean with my ex, leaving my so-called girlfriend behind. Was there a way back from this? Did I want it?

Hayley reappeared with a book adorned with a glossy pink stiletto on the front. "You can borrow it when I'm done if you want," she said with a wink.

"Yeah, thanks. Not sure it's my style, but hey, I may get bored I suppose."

"Not with me around. Non-stop fun, remember?" I looked over at her, but her nose was already into her book.

Chapter 15

We went for a stroll into the small town for lunch one day, and settled underneath an umbrella to shelter us from the midday sun.

"So what about you then?" I pointed at Hayley. "Who have you been seeing back home? There's always someone."

"I don't know what you mean."

"Please, always the woman of mystery. You even hinted at it when I saw you at the café the other week." I said.

"Did I? Well, I don't know. How about you? What happened with Sara? I get the impression this was more than just a fling."

I looked down at the plates of tapas that divided us. "I thought it was."

"But she let you down."

"Maybe. I don't know. Would I have done the same in her position? Perhaps."

"Oh come on, Cameron, I saw the state you were in after she called. She made it very clear where her priorities lay."

"Well, wouldn't you? She's known me for a couple of months, she's spent her life building her political career." I felt myself bristling at the veiled criticism.

"Don't make excuses for her," said Hayley with a fire in her eyes I hadn't seen before. "She's a fool. It didn't have to be as clear cut as you or her career. She could have sorted it out."

"Perhaps." I felt the backs of my eyes grow hot, and I swallowed hurriedly, not wanting to cry in such a public place. We had been in Ibiza now for several days, but still the thought of Sara caught me unawares. "I don't know, Hayley, I really don't. I know I loved her."

"You loved her?"

"I think so. She said she loved me too."

"It's not only about what you say though. What about actions?"

"Ok. I'm going to the loo. When I get back we need to talk about something else." As I stood Hayley laid a hand on my forearm. I looked at her briefly before heading into the café.

When I returned I found my wine glass had been refilled, and Hayley was chasing an olive around a plate with a cocktail stick. I smiled at her before I spoke. "I still don't get olives. I mean really, what is the point of them?" I asked as I sat down.

"That's because you have no sophistication my dear. One day you will understand olives and all the mysteries of love." Hayley's voice was gentle, as though she was trying to convey more than just the words she spoke.

"I hold out very little hope of either of those things, but I admire your optimism. Wine however, I do understand. Look at the colour of that rosé. Beautiful."

"Notes of cedar, darling?"

I swirled my glass and laughed. "Oh definitely, and undertones of new car."

"Gorgeous."

Warmed by the sun, and comfortably relaxed by the wine, we returned to our room later that day after a light dinner in the hotel. "Come on, Cam, come out onto the balcony with me."

"God, the sun going down over there looks gorgeous doesn't it?" I felt the warmth of Hayley next to me, and relaxation gave way to something else.

"I need to tell you something," said Hayley, placing her hand once again on my forearm. "I should have said it sooner, but I know you're still getting over Sara and all that crap back in the UK." I turned slightly towards her, the fading light placing her face in shadow. I drew my arm back and let her hand fall into mine.

"Tell me." I felt my pulse quicken, and a flow of warmth through my chest.

"I didn't mean it to go so far, or for things to be so serious. Everything happened so quickly with you, with me, with everything."

"I'm not sure I understand what you mean," I said, gently stroking her thumb with my own, enjoying the sensation, pressing the mute button on everything else in my life.

"Sorry, Cam, I know, I'm not really making sense." Hayley drew her free hand through her hair and sighed. "You asked me earlier whether there was anyone."

"If you're trying to tell me you have someone or other you're dating," I said, swallowing, "then don't worry. I know that you always have someone somewhere."

Hayley frowned. "There is someone. But he's not a 'someone or other'."

"He?"

"Yeah. He asked me to marry him." I gripped the balcony with one hand, and stilled the hand that held hers.

"He proposed?"

"Yes." I could feel my heart rate soar, and somewhere in my head I was curious to know why. Somewhere in my body there was an answer I wasn't prepared to listen to.

"When?"

"The night before I came over to yours." I wasn't sure what to say, so I stayed silent. "He asked me then." I withdrew my hand and placed it into the pocket of my jeans.

"What did you say?" I asked, not sure which answer I was hoping for.

"I said I'd think about it."

"Really?" She looked down and nodded. "You mean you're actually considering it? You? Married?"

"Honestly? I don't know." In the distance I could hear gentle waves against the hull of a boat that had been moored for the evening.

"Does he know you're here?" She nodded. "With me?"

"Yes, but," she trailed off.

"He doesn't know we were together."

"It's not like you've told Sara anything though is it?" she said, and I sensed a trace of defensiveness in her tone.

"That's different," I said petulantly.

"And anyway, we're friends." She motioned to me. "There's nothing going on." I felt an evening breeze begin to rise.

"No, nothing." I stopped. "Do you love him?"

"Oh don't ask me that." Hayley put a hand over her face. Part of me wanted to take her into my arms and comfort her. The other part of me felt less sympathetic.

"That poor bloke," I said quietly. Then I looked up at her. "If it hadn't been for him proposing, would you even have come to see me, or suggested us coming away? Is this just you running away masquerading as friendship?" There was a long pause.

"I'm going to bed."

"Hayley, please, don't you think we should talk about this?"

"Look, Cam, I don't know ok, all the questions you ask, I just don't know. I'm not deliberately trying to annoy you."

"Annoy me?" I said, traces of anger in my voice. "You think this is about annoying me? God you haven't changed have you."

Hayley kept to her own side of the bed that night, and I didn't sleep well. It was after 2am by the time I properly slept, thoughts of Hayley, her mystery man and Sara swirling in my head.

Chapter 16

"Cameron, darling, wake up. You can't sleep the day away." I stirred, feeling Hayley's soft hand on my shoulder. "It's gone 11." I grunted, pleased of the excuse of just waking up not to have to converse in any meaningful way. "I'll go down to the bar for a coffee for you while you wake up."

I watched her figure retreat. The aroma of her freshly shampooed hair and expensive sun cream remained. I shook my head and sighed. There was something conciliatory about her actions. "What am I doing?" I asked out loud to no one in particular. I suspected either Sara or Hayley could give me an answer, but neither would get it right. My own answer would probably make even less sense.

I turned onto my back and stretched out my arms. I was torn between wanting to know why she had really come away with me, wanting to know who he was, and never wanting to hear of him again. I poked a foot out from under the covers, and allowed it to bathe in a pillar of sunshine shooting through the curtains. She was right, I couldn't sleep the day away. I pulled myself up and sat on the balcony which was already baking, and soothed my muddled head.

"Here you are," said Hayley, sitting down opposite me, and putting my coffee on the small table between us. She had one too. "I'm sorry, Cam, I should have been honest with you from the start."

"No, it's fine, you don't owe me an explanation. It's your life."

"I know, but I guess because of what's happening and us, and being away," she said. I interrupted her before she could continue.

"Yeah, yes, it is different. But we are our own people. I think it's just I'm a bit sensitive right now. And back when we were together, you couldn't even have that conversation. You couldn't begin to consider the future, what it might hold, if we could be in it." I sipped the coffee, which was bitter, cutting through the stale sleepy taste in my mouth.

"I know, Cam. I'm not good at this stuff. Max has had his fair share of that too." I felt my stomach lurch slightly. He had a name. I wasn't sure why that made me feel bad.

"What will you tell him?"

"I really don't know. I can't think about it. It's hard to think about him here." She gestured to the space around her. I wasn't sure if she meant being with me, or being in Ibiza.

"Maybe that's why you're here?" No one spoke for a moment. "You can't run forever."

"No." She looked up at me, and the complexity of how I felt quadrupled. Part of me hated it. But deep down, part of me couldn't resist it.

"All right, Hayley, I won't put you on the spot any more. What are we going to do today?"

"Beach, book and beer I think." I nodded my agreement and we hit the sun loungers.

A few days later Hayley handed me a leaflet. "How about this? A sunset cruise around San Antonio – starts mid-afternoon, includes food on board, and champagne at sea."

"Irresistible," I said.

"I thought so."

Until then we laid by the pool side by side, reading, not talking – something we had done a lot of. It was comfortable and undemanding.

The sun beat down on us as we stood on the jetty in the heat of the day waiting for our boat. "God that hat looks ridiculous," I said. Hayley pouted from underneath the large floppy straw hat she had bought herself in a tat-filled shop along the sea front. Somehow she managed to make it look elegant. I made do with a scarf to protect my head.

"Yeah, well at least I don't look like a pirate," she said.

I slapped my thigh. "Arrrr!" We began to attract glances from the others waiting on the tiny wooden pier and giggled. "Perhaps more Captain Pugwash than Captain Jack? Ooh look, is that ours?" I asked, pointing out to sea. Coming into the bay we could see a medium sized wooden vessel, complete with mast and sails gliding over the mirrored water.

"Beautiful," said Hayley, lifting the front of her hat up, which had flopped down over her eyes momentarily. "Perhaps I should have dressed like a pirate too. Have you seen the flag?" There was a skull and cross bones atop the mast.

"I always was a fashion icon," I said, gathering my possessions. The gracefulness of the ship belied its speed, and it wasn't long before it was moored by the jetty and beginning to take on passengers.

We teetered up the rickety gangway, and found ourselves some seats in the shade on deck. Soon, we were speeding out of the bay around the coast of the island.

The welcome breeze blew Hayley's hair into my face, her hat now stuffed back into her bag. I gathered the wayward fronds of hair in my hands and held them together in a ponytail behind her head, smoothing it backwards. I grabbed my scarf and tied it around her head to tame her curls.

"Thanks, darling. You always did look after me so well."

"Did I?" I asked, genuinely. She cocked her head to one side. "I'm not sure you really wanted looking after."

"Maybe not. He wants to look after me." She didn't need to tell me who 'he' was.

"And you're not keen to let him?" She looked away.

"I'm not ready."

"Will you ever be?"

"Good question. I really don't know. You would have taken care of me wouldn't you?" She looked back at me, her eyes dark.

The sea spray was salty on my tongue.

"Is it wise to revisit this stuff, Hayley?" I said quietly.

"Who bloody knows what's wise. Did she look after you?" It was my turn to look away.

"Yes, she did."

"Until..."

I spoke before she could say any more. "Until. But I suppose that's the risk you take. Right?"

"Well, the risk you take perhaps, but not me."

"And you're happier for it are you?"

"Touché." We sat in silence for a while, watching the waves lap against the side of the golden brown varnished side of the boat. Here and there a pink jellyfish would appear and then vanish into the blue green depths. There was a beauty about the creatures, although the locals had warned us to avoid them when swimming due to their fearsome stinging potential.

The afternoon turned into evening, and the sky began to change colour. There was something magnetic about the horizon as we watched the sun begin to go down. We stood, side by side, leaning against the side of the boat, drinking in the sight before us. It had been a relaxing day and we had spent most of it reading and sunbathing on deck. Glasses of champagne were pressed into our hands by the crew, and chill-out music played, giving pathos to the setting sun, making this daily occurrence into an epic drama played out for our gratification.

I turned my head and saw Hayley gazing out to sea, oblivious to me. I allowed myself to wonder what might have been, had she allowed our relationship back then to continue, had she not backed away. She was lit in red and purple by the setting sun, and with the lapping sea and music, there was something irresistible about the thought of 'what if'. We were so far from everyone and everything else – Sara, Tom, Hayley's husband-in-waiting. None of them mattered any more.

She turned her head towards me, and smiled. She rested her hand on mine. "It's beautiful isn't it?"

A seagull flew across the giant red orb of the sun, as it sank ever lower. It touched the sea, and I half expected to hear a sizzle as it met the cool water.

"I'm trying to work out who is running away here," I said quietly. "You, or me?"

Hayley laughed quietly. "Maybe we both are?"

"I know one thing. I need to stop thinking so much." I said, enjoying the weightless feeling the champagne was giving me.

"I'll second that," she said, draining her champagne glass and placing it by her feet. The sun was a half circle and disappearing fast into the ocean. Our faces were close enough to touch, and by some unspoken agreement we moved together. Our lips touched and we kissed. There was something real, reassuring and powerful about it. Her hands came up to my hair and I rested mine on her hips.

As we parted, we saw the last glint of sunlight dip into the sea, and we knew this meant the party at San Antonio had just begun. The boat turned and sailed into shore. Half an hour later we sat at a small table opposite one another, looking out at the deep blue sky and inky sea. I licked my lips, which tasted of champagne and sea spray. Hayley smiled at me, "Well I'm glad we're not staying on this side of the island. Don't drink that beer too quickly, I had to sell a kidney to buy it." I laughed. The music was loud, with a driving bass line, and we were surrounded by groups of people clearly out on what could only be described as a big night.

"I'm not sure we're cool enough for this crowd," I said, looking around at the super-slim, expensively dressed images of youthful perfection around us.

"Speak for yourself. What we lack in style, we make up for in intelligence and humour, Cam. Now I don't know about you, but I don't fancy a night on the tiles. Once we've had these, shall we head back for a nightcap at the hotel?"

"Thank God. I was worried you were going to make me pay 50 Euros to get into Pascha. I'm sure it's amazing, but I know I'd just end up complaining we couldn't hear each other speak." I was genuinely relieved. There was a tension between us and it could no longer be ignored.

"Maybe you're right, perhaps we're not cool enough for this place. I don't really care though. It's been a lovely day hasn't it?" Hayley smiled at me.

"Yeah, really nice. You can't beat a boat, good music, sunset,"

"And good company."

"Well, I suppose." Hayley jabbed my arm and we both laughed.

"Here's to running away," she said, raising her glass to mine.

"And arriving here."

It wasn't long before we were in a taxi, speeding across the island back to our home from home. We were dropped outside the front of our hotel. The idea of going into the confined space of our room felt a bit overwhelming though.

"Walk on the beach?" I asked. We walked down the steps onto the silky white sand. I let Hayley take my hand and we strolled along the water's edge. "This really is just perfection." She squeezed my hand.

"No less than you deserve, Cameron," she said. She stopped, and pulled me round to face her. She took my other hand, and then placed my arms around her. "Kiss me, Cameron. Please." So I did. It was no hardship. There was something fantastical about this place, and with her mouth, more keenly on mine this time, I was fully transported. My fingers savoured the feel of the warm skin on her back, and I pulled her closer, my tongue touching her lips. She ran her fingers through my hair and I felt my stomach flip.

"I want you," I said, simply.

Hayley smiled, and rested her forehead on mine. "You've got me."

"No, I really want you, Hayley."

"On the beach?"

"That sort of thing only works on TV – have you seen how fine the sand is?" I gesticulated as I spoke She threw her head back and laughed.

"Come on, cautious Cameron. Take me home." I took her hand and we walked back towards the hotel. We stood in the lift, side by side, facing the mirror. The journey to the third floor took an agonisingly long time. I urged it to go quicker before the world started to invade my senses once more. I was determined to just feel, and not think. The air was still and close in the small space, and from the connection of our hands the heat seemed to intensify. I looked at the floor, nothing in my mind but her mouth on mine, and the visceral sensations she had awakened in me. She drew her thumb across my wrist, as we passed the first floor, and I felt a spark travel down my legs. I laced my fingers through hers and brought my thumb to her palm in a caress that felt unlikely in its intimacy. I heard Hayley gently breathe out and I looked up into the mirror for the first time. She was looking back at my reflection. We passed the second floor and I turned my head and looked at her bare neck, displayed perfectly by her halter top. I could smell her perfume and found myself stifling a sigh. The lift arrived at floor three, and by silent agreement we walked swiftly to our room. I fumbled with the key card. Hayley placed her hand over mine, took the card from me, and put it cleanly into the slot. The lock mechanism clicked open and she pushed open the door. I followed her in, letting the door close behind me. She turned to face me. I placed my hands on her hips and walked her backwards towards the wall. I pressed the length of my body against hers and looked at her eyes, which were dark and beckoning. I pressed my lips to hers in a kiss that released all the tension that I had been feeling in the last week. It was a long, passionate kiss, our tongues meeting and exploring and teasing. It was reckless and raw and destructive and I didn't care. Her hands rested at the base of my spine, sending sensual messages to my brain. All my nerves were exposed when she started to gently kiss my neck. I brought my hands up to her sides, and allowed my thumb to graze her breast. I heard my own sigh, as I brought my hands up behind her neck, untied the straps of her top, and pulled it down. Her bare, braless skin was too inviting to resist, and I brought my mouth to her erect nipple. I felt her breath quicken on the back of my neck, and brought my face to meet hers and we kissed hungrily, not wanting the moment to end. Without breaking the contact between our lips, she took my right hand and placed it between her legs. I could feel her need for me through the cotton of her knickers. I softly stroked her and she urged me on with her sighs. Pulling the material to one side, I could feel how ready she was for me, and pressed my fingers into her, her body tensing as I did, and her breathing becoming heavier. "Yes," she whispered. I found her most sensitive spot and began to massage it slowly but firmly, her breath coming more irregularly now, in gasps. "More," she said in a breathlessly, and I was powerless to deny her, my own breathing becoming quicker, as I pushed inside her, our bodies ever closer together, as we rocked against the wall. I braced her as her sighs rose into groans of pleasure and her thighs twitched. I brought my other hand back up to her breast, and stroked it, sending her over the edge into an orgasm that announced itself with a single cry from Hayley. I felt her muscles tighten around my fingers, and her body tensed against mine for almost a minute.

As she relaxed, I took her in my arms and gently kissed her. Her eyes, which had been tightly shut since we'd started kissing, opened a crack. "God you're good," she said, with a lazy grin. I smiled, acutely aware of my own need to feel her against my naked body.

"I'm still fully clothed," I whispered in her ear.

"Give me a minute, Cam. You can't do that to a girl and expect her to recover in the blink of an eye." We both laughed, and kissed, and laughed some more. I took her hand and guided her to the bed. She star-fished on the bed and I tucked myself into a small space next to her. "Ok," she said, "I think I may need more than a minute."

Our hands were still connected, and we lay in silence for several minutes. I allowed my eyes to close, and the drowsiness of the alcohol made my mind swim. That weekend in the Lake District, the wine, the conversation, the connection, the affection in her eyes. Fingers slowly crept up my wrist. I sighed. "Don't go to sleep, Cameron, I have plans for you." Hayley's voice came from Sara's mouth in my imagination. I shook my head.

"As if I could fall asleep." I pushed out a smile. "Give me a minute gorgeous." I padded over to the mini bar and found myself a bottle of chilled water. My throat contracted as the icy contents poured down. A shock to the system. Something to awaken me from my drifting. The more I tried not to think about Sara, the more she appeared in my head, fully formed, wearing beautiful clothes and smelling amazing. There she was, propped up against the door frame, smiling a wistful, knowing smile. A smile of forgiveness. Wishful thinking. I shook my head again.

"You all right, Cam?" asked Hayley, who had propped herself up on an elbow.

"Yeah." Even I was unconvinced.

"What's with the water? I think we need something stronger. What's in there?"

I looked inside the mini bar once again and retrieved two bottles of European beer. "I'm ok, just tired."

"Not too tired I hope?" She took a beer from me, had a sip and placed it on the bedside cabinet. I downed half my bottle and did the same. I climbed back onto the bed. "You were always a mystery weren't you?" she said.

"I'm not sure I was," I said quietly.

"I never worked you out babe." She smiled. There was no malice in her voice, just a gentle sadness. "Stop thinking so much, Cam. Let's have this moment. Just now, just tonight." She put her hand on my thigh. "The future will take care of itself."

I took another liberal swig from my beer. She was right. All we had was now. I exhaled, leaned down and kissed her. Within seconds she had flipped me onto my back and she was on top of me. There was a caution and softness in the way she handled me. Perhaps she understood me perfectly after all.

Our lovemaking was languid, familiar and respectful. The earlier passion had made way for something deeper. Something closer to love. A love that had never quite come to pass.

Chapter 17

I woke up before Hayley did the following morning. I watched her breath rise and fall in her chest as she slept. Her hair was spread across the pillow, and I ran my fingers gently along the locks, taking in their softness. Oblivious to my distant touch she slept on. Her left hand had been flung in her unconsciousness above her head on the pillow. I wondered if she had an engagement ring. She wasn't wearing it. Was it here? In her suitcase? I wondered whether it was in a drawer at home. Maybe there wasn't a ring yet. Perhaps he'd proposed in a moment of spontaneous love. I could understand that. The sheets had been flung off in the heat of the night. Her legs were arranged as if running. I found myself feeling sorry for Max. What kind of future could he hope for with Hayley now?

The fingers of her hand clenched and she stretched out her arm. She didn't open her eyes. "How long have you been watching me?"

"Your eyes are closed, you have no idea what I'm doing. I could be stealing all your worldly belongings for all you know."

She opened one eye. "Nope. I was right. Was I snoring?"

"No, you were very peaceful," I said. She closed her eyes again and smiled.

"Last day," she said.

"Yeah." I had been dimly aware of this fact the previous night. I hadn't allowed myself to think of it until now. "Remind me what time your flight is?" I already knew that it was at 10pm, but played for time before I worked out what my response should be. She answered sleepily, and then rolled over onto her back. Her eyes opened once again, blearily.

"This week's gone quickly." It was a statement, not a question. I pursed my lips together. This was goodbye.

"Is he picking you up from the airport?" I asked, immediately hating myself for saying it out loud.

There was a long pause, which told me all I needed to know. It wasn't a surprise, and in many ways I'd have been surprised if she had denied it. "He asked if he could."

"What will you tell him?"

"I don't know yet." She closed her eyes again. I closed mine. I wondered whether I would get an invitation to the wedding. I got out of bed and headed towards the shower. She made no move to follow me or call me back.

I washed off the evidence of the night we had shared. The events were increasingly feeling like a dream. Whether it was a good or bad dream, I couldn't decide. But a dream nonetheless. She was ready to go home to her life. I wasn't sure what awaited me. I had another week of this particular reverie. I wasn't sure whether that was something I genuinely wanted. But what would reality bring? I wasn't sure about that either.

We went down to breakfast together once we had both showered. The smorgasbord of goodies that awaited us was a welcome diversion. I allowed the chef to make me a pile of crepes, which I devoured, accompanied by Nutella and fresh fruit. Hayley stuck to her usual cereal and toast, but I noticed she had more of both. I thought about making a joke about building up an appetite. Somehow it didn't feel appropriate. Although I was beginning to lose grip on what was and was not appropriate any more. I was, after all, the 'donations for sex' girl. For the first time I allowed myself an inward smile at this fact. Being away from the UK, and avoiding all British papers since we'd been away had done me good. The inward smile fell as soon as it had risen though. How was Sara dealing with things? Were the papers still as intense? She was always much more of a target than I was.

We spent the rest of the day on sun loungers on the beach reading our respective books. It felt as though we had said everything that needed saying. I didn't go with her to the airport, she didn't want me to. When her taxi arrived to take her there from the hotel, I wrapped her in my arms and we kissed. It felt right. I savoured the feel of her hand at the back of my head, and ran my fingers through the ends of her tousled hair. We parted and she looked at me without speaking for a while.

"Thank you," she said. I'm not sure what for. But I nodded, unable to think of an appropriate response. As she climbed into the taxi, I felt a stab of fear for what was next. Now I truly was alone. Perhaps more than I had ever been.

The car pulled away. I watched the rear lights fade into the night. "Good bye," I said, to the cool darkness around me.

I slept well that night. I surprised myself by waking in a good mood. I went to breakfast early, bought a newspaper, and ordered more pancakes. It was time to face the music. I made sure I'd had at least one cup of tea before I allowed myself to look carefully at the British paper. On the front page of the red top I had selected was a story about a reality TV star I had never heard of. I allowed myself to relax a little. It wasn't until the fifth page that I saw a story that rang a bell. There had been machinations in Sara's party, and some talk of a leadership challenge. Her name was mentioned as a potential challenger. I sighed when I saw that it came alongside the words 'recently disgraced' and 'rehabilitation of her career'. I felt a stab of guilt. Perhaps it was all my fault. There was a picture of her outside the Commons. It was grainy and small, and I couldn't work out how recent it was. She was looking away from the camera and smiling at someone out of shot. I wondered who it was. I hoped she didn't regret the short time we'd shared. I didn't. There were other things I regretted far more.

I caught up with the rest of the goings on as I drank more coffee than was sensible. I was intrigued by the story about the leadership challenge though. It was well known that there were concerns about the current leader of the opposition and his electability. A General Election was likely to be looming, so it sounded like one or two people were getting cold feet. I allowed myself to imagine Sara leaning on the dispatch box opposite the Prime Minister. I smiled at the thought.

The days after that passed in a blur of good food, crime novels, sunshine and the odd glass of wine. I grew used to my own company, even relishing it as the week wore on. I began trying to make a plan for my return. I started to think about the future again. I still didn't know what I would do, now I was unemployed. But while I was watching the sun set over the sea one evening, I realised I was beginning to see that as an opportunity. There were no expectations. I had no ties. I could do whatever I wanted.

Chapter 18

When the wheels of my plane touched down in the UK it was, inevitably, raining. The air that greeted me on the steps down to the tarmac was fresh and clean. I was home. I sped through passport control to pick up my luggage, and then jumped into the first available cab. It was growing dark as I was driven through my home town. I was hypnotised by headlights, tail lights and windscreen wipers.

Home was a welcome sight. Having left with barely a glance at my front door, I was pleased to see it once again. I touched the brass numbers on the door and smiled to myself. It had been quite a fortnight. I placed my key into the lock, and let myself back in. There was a modest pile of post on the doormat, which I kicked to one side. Before I did anything else I wanted a cup of tea. There was something odd about tea anywhere but in the UK, which I realise made me sound like a walking stereotype. I managed to find a bourbon biscuit to go with the tea – the perfect antidote to some of the extravagant dishes I had been eating in Ibiza. I sat down in the living room, and appreciated my beautifully sprung sofa like never before. There was nothing like a flight to remind you of the comforts in life. I embraced my Englishness, and popped my feet up beside me on the sofa. It was good to be home.

I put the television on. A medical drama filled the screen, and there was something soothing about the mundanity of it. The lack of glamour, heat and sunshine was homely.

It was an hour or so later that I took my suitcase from the hallway into the bedroom where I found my shattered phone. I looked at it once, and then walked into the kitchen. I retrieved a dustpan and brush from under the sink and returned to the mess. I swept it up, poured it into some old newspaper, wrapped it up and threw it away. I needed a new phone. A new number too. Decision made, pan and brush replaced, I went to bed.

The next morning I picked up the small pile of post on my way out, stuffing it into my bag for later.

The bus into town took me through the grey streets of my city. I walked anonymously down the high street to a bright white mobile phone shop. I was ready to reconnect.

I visited a coffee shop over the road, where I could sit in the window and people watch, while setting up my new piece of kit. The knowledge that as yet no one had my number was both lonely and thrilling. I put in all the requisite codes, and for the first time in a fortnight logged into my email account. 59 new messages. I scrolled through them, dismissing the countless advertisements and sales messages. There were a couple of emails from HR at the university, confirming the details of the end of my contract. I needed to sign some kind of non-disclosure paperwork. I frowned. There was one from Simon too. Rather sweetly, he was asking how I was getting on, and confirming that media requests had died down from his end. I felt strangely warm towards the man who had invaded my flat in the midst of all the drama in order to protect my former employer. I sent a few words of thanks, and let him know I was ok.

My stomach lurched when I saw the next email. It was Tom. He had sent it just a day after I'd left for Ibiza. The anger was still there, but it was cooler, mellower. The wound had begun to heal. I wasn't sure I wanted to open it though. I drank some of the sweet, strong flavoured coffee I'd treated myself to, took a deep breath, and tapped the message with my index finger.

Dear Cam,

God that sounds formal. Sorry. Cam. I am sorry. I know I said it on the phone. But I wanted to write it down. I want to make sure I have done all I can do to let you know that I deeply regret what I did. I was stupid, foolish and drunk. I was trying to impress him. I doubt it helps you to know that I've told him I won't see him again. But I have.

I tried to call you back so many times. I don't blame you for switching off your phone or blocking me or whatever you did. I even came to your flat, but you didn't answer the door. Or maybe you weren't in. That's why I'm emailing you. I know you might delete it or just ignore it. I'm not trying to make excuses and I don't expect immediate forgiveness. But I just want you to know that I love you. You're my best friend. I can't bear to think about my life without you. There's a gin and tonic by my laptop as I type, but I can't even enjoy that without you to drink it with.

So, through my gin addled meanderings, I hereby make you a promise. I won't phone you, I'll stop coming to your flat and knocking on your door. I won't send you any emails after this one either. But I promise you, that however long it takes you, when you are ready, I will still be here, waiting for you. If it takes weeks, months, years, whatever. You know where I am. Knock on my door, any time, day or night. Email me, call me. I don't care. But when that moment comes – if it comes – I'll be waiting for you, Cam.

With all my love

Tom xxx

I put the phone down. There was a charm to his words. The fact they made me smile, and well up a little bit, irritated me. I rolled my eyes at myself and laughed quietly. Bloody Tom. Such an idiot. I hit 'reply'.

Tom, you're a total drama queen. I've got a new number. Here it is – call me. C x

I pressed send, a frisson of hope surging through me. Maybe it had just been a drunken whim. Perhaps he'd moved on. It had been two weeks. I drained my coffee and ordered another. I looked at the remainder of my inbox. There was another name I was looking for, even though I pretended I wasn't. A name whose absence made my eyes well up again. I bit my lip. The second coffee was strong and bitter. It was welcome. I swallowed down my tears. My phone lit up and started to ring with a generic ring tone.

"That was quick," I said, trying to exude flippancy. There was a pause on the line. I heard him take a breath.

"Hi."

"Hi," I replied. "I got your email." I shook my head at the awkwardness of my answer after such a cavalier start.

"I'm sorry, Cam."

"I know, Tom. Look, let's not do this on the phone. I'm right by you. Come and meet me."

I was nervous to think I would be seeing him again, but I was excited too. It was time I had my friend back. I drained the second coffee. My hands shook and I was bobbing my knee up and down thanks to the caffeine. I took my empty mugs to the counter and ordered a peppermint tea. Something that would hopefully sooth the nervous energy rising within me. I picked up a muffin too, hoping it would stop my stomach swirling in apprehension.

As I sat back down, a felt a hand on my shoulder. "God, you must have sprinted here," I said, jumping.

"Pretty much," panted Tom. He stiffly took a seat next to me, unable to look me in the eye.

"You look a bit pale, perhaps we should share this?" I proffered the blueberry muffin.

"Thanks, darling. I might just grab a flat white first."

By the time he returned to his seat he seemed calmer. He smiled. We both paused. I wanted to hug him. But it didn't feel right somehow.

"I am sorry, Cam. I was an idiot."

"I know, Tom." I took his hand. "It's ok." His head dropped.

"But it's not though is it? You've lost your job."

"And Sara. But if it hadn't been you, someone else would have blabbed. I miss you. I want my friend back." I squeezed his hand. He gave a weak smile.

"Where have you been? You look like you've been in the sun." It was my turn to smile.

"Ibiza. Got back last night."

"Oh I see, you really did get away from it all didn't you?" He withdrew his hand to start dividing the muffin.

"Yeah."

"Alone?" I bit my lip. "Oh, hello… Who were you with? It can't have been Sara, I saw her on the news last week." I shook my head. "Who?"

"Hayley."

"Hayley? Hayley who broke your heart? Oh my God, Cam, where did she come from?"

"She was just there. I was alone, I'd lost everything, and everyone. And she was there."

Tom looked away.

"I'm glad you weren't alone," he said softly. "I wish I could have been there." We watched the people going past for a few moments. "What about Sara?"

I shrugged. "I don't know. She had to pull back to save her career I guess. I've not heard from her."

"Not at all?" He raised his eyebrows. "That surprises me. She didn't seem like the sort to cut and run."

I felt the corners of my mouth turn down. "No, she didn't."

"What are you going to do now?"

"I really don't know, Tom. I need to start thinking about finding a job I suppose. Not sure who'll want me now though."

Tom shook his head. "Don't worry, people have short memories. You're good at what you do, don't sell yourself short."

"I hope you're right."

"So what did you get up to in Ibiza?" He asked, stirring a sugar into his coffee. My cheeks flushed. "Oh my God, you slept with her didn't you? Are you seeing her? You hussy!"

I laughed. "Steady on. I'm not seeing her."

"But you did sleep with her didn't you?"

"Perhaps." I stuffed some muffin into my mouth.

"You dirty dog! Was it good?" I pointed to my full mouth in response, trying to avoid the question, but Tom could read the colour of my face. "Well, why the hell not? Good for you."

We both paused for a few moments. I was reassured at how relaxed things felt between us. His humility had touched me.

"Are you ok though?" he asked me, a serious look on his face.

"Well, yes, I think I am surprisingly enough. I mean, I'm not ecstatic, I don't wake up every morning on a total high. But I do wake up every morning aware of the opportunity I have. I feel sad about what happened with Sara. I miss her. But, I don't know, she feels like she's from another world now. As for work, I don't know what I'm going to do yet, but I still have a bit of thinking time."

"There's a lot of call for your skills in the industry."

"To be honest, Tom, it feels like a chance for me to move on and do something different. Besides, I used to be plagued by recruitment consultants inviting me to apply for similar jobs in all sorts of places, but since the shit hit the fan I've not heard a whisper. I think I've burned my bridges in the university world. Cameron Strawbank," I said, as though my name was in lights, "scarlet woman."

"I'm sorry."

"Honestly, Tom, don't be. I think I'm done with mixing with people who are so far removed from the real world. I've had enough of traipsing down to London to see how the other half lives. As I walked down here this afternoon I saw nine people sleeping rough in the space of less than 200 metres."

Tom nodded. "It's definitely got worse recently."

"Maybe I need to do something in my own community, my own city. God knows what though."

"There won't be big bucks in it," said Tom. I shrugged.

"Beyond a certain point, as long as I can pay my bills and occasionally go on holiday, I'm not sure that matters to me." I finished off the muffin. "Although when I'm on the breadline this time next year, you can tell me you told me so." We laughed, and it felt good.

"But about Sara..." began Tom. I rolled my eyes. "You don't want to speak to her? Get some kind of closure at least?" He shifted in his seat. "I saw the way you looked at each other. You loved each other."

A sadness pulled at me from my stomach. "Maybe you're right. I don't even have her number any more though. My old phone broke."

"Wow, bad timing. I wondered why you had a new number." I shrugged again. He didn't need the full story, or his particular part in it. "So she could be ringing you every day and assuming you're ignoring her, but actually it's just that your phone's knackered?"

"I don't think she is," I said, as much to myself as to Tom.

"It wouldn't be too hard to contact her though – remember I have the college database at my fingertips." I looked at him, and he shrugged. He knew I wanted to change the subject.

"How are things at work?" I asked.

"Well, for a week it was, of course, all about you and what Damien is calling 'Cam's indiscretion'."

"Ha, I really do sound like a scarlet woman now."

"Yeah, he spent days in and out of meetings with the External Affairs Director and the Vice Chancellor looking very serious and channelling 'importance' and 'problem solver'." I laughed at Tom's air quotes.

"I can imagine. Have you started recruiting for my replacement?"

"Not yet. I imagine a reshuffle is imminent. You know what it's like, always a chance to re-organise and promote those deserving souls who have scratched his back in the last year or so." Tom rolled his eyes. "I'm not sure I want to stay. It's not the same without you. And after what happened I feel like I really shouldn't be there."

"Oh, Tom, you can't sacrifice your career for me. It's like I said, this has forced me to think about a different path for myself."

"Maybe it's time for a new path for me too," he said, thoughtfully, gazing out of the window at the crowds passing by.

"Well just promise me you won't rush into anything," I said, "Tom, look at me, promise me."

Tom turned, smiled, took my hand and said, "I hereby solemnly swear not to rush into anything. God, where has this new wise owl Cam come from? What happened to you in Ibiza? Actually, no, I don't want to know about your sordid lady-loving ways."

We passed another half an hour catching up. We parted agreeing to meet up in a few days for dinner. I smiled all the way home. It was the first time I'd put into words how I was feeling. I really did have a big opportunity now, although as yet what it looked like, I did not know.

Chapter 19

I spent the next few days taking the opportunity to give my apartment a thorough spring clean. I sorted cupboards, threw out clothes I never wore and even defrosted the freezer. I'd never done it before, and had to google instructions. It truly was a new start.

I did a thorough hoover of the whole apartment one afternoon, and nudged my bag as I did. Several letters fell out, and I remembered I hadn't yet read through my post since being away. I had been side-tracked by Tom's appearance. I killed the power and picked up the bundle of post, settling down on my beloved sofa. Inevitably there were several bills and junk mail. There was also some paperwork I needed to sign from the college. I set it aside so as not to forget. The sooner I formally cut my ties, the happier I would be. That episode in my life was closed.

The last letter had a handwritten envelope, a curiously unusual occurrence in these days of digital communication. The postmark was Westminster, leaving me in no doubt as to who it was from. I set it down on my lap and clasped my hands together. I wasn't sure what to expect. I picked it up again and examined that postmark. It had been posted just over a week before. I smiled remembering Sara telling me that Westminster had its own post office and postmark, and that one day she would send something to me with it on. My eyes filled with tears. I hadn't imagined this would be our situation as and when she did it. I turned over the envelope and tore it open. Out came a card, with a picture of a poppy field on. Beautiful blue sky, green meadow and red poppies undulating in the wind.

Her handwriting was as gorgeous as I remembered it from that cheque she wrote the first time I met her. Was it possible to be attracted to someone based only on their handwriting? I was beginning to feel it was.

Dear Cameron,

First, how are you? I've tried to call you, but your number stopped working last week. I really want to talk to you. I'm so sorry for how things have ended up. That day was such a mess. And I feel responsible.

I want you to know that I was never casual about us. I meant everything I said to you. It was never meant to end this way. I wonder whether you might be able to forgive me for what happened? I tried to explain myself at the time, but I know I didn't do a very good job. I would like it if we could meet, even if it is just one more time. I want to see you for myself, check you are ok.

I totally understand if you don't want to see me again. I knew what I was getting into becoming an MP, entering into public life. This is the risk I perpetually take. But you didn't sign up for that. I don't know how it got out, but it did. And really, if I'm being frank with you, I should have been readier for that than I was. I should have warned you of the risks.

You know where I am. Call me.

With my love,

Sara

Her number was neatly written at the bottom. I wiped the tears from my eyes and stifled a sob. For the last two weeks I had kept myself sane by imagining that it hadn't been as good with her as it really had been. But this note was her down to the ground. She was sorry, she cared, and she wanted to talk to me. It felt obvious that we were never going to rekindle what we once had. She herself referred to it having ended. But she wanted closure too. I wasn't sure I could face seeing her, but I also knew it probably wasn't a conversation that should happen over the phone. After a lot of thought I composed a simple text. I suggested meeting in a couple of days' time in London. I didn't expect an immediate response, knowing her timetable was so packed, and if she really was considering some kind of run for party leadership, I doubted I would be figuring much in her life. I almost leapt off my seat, when just three minutes later my phone pinged to let me know she had responded. I felt a chill travel down from my head to my Converse clad feet. She didn't say much, but she suggested a time and I swiftly responded with my agreement.

I continued to feel jittery for the rest of the day, so I decided to go for a walk. I passed a church hall that was advertising a summer fête in aid of some local charity. I had nothing else to do, so I wandered in. There was something quintessential about the bunting and the fairy cakes and the round men and women in cardigans. I went over to the cake stall and bought myself a tea loaf that I'd be able to eke out for the rest of the week with my afternoon cuppa in front of Countdown, something which was rapidly becoming something of a routine. Not one that I would advertise of course, but enjoyable nonetheless. I was perusing the home made jams on the neighbouring stall when I heard a familiar voice. "I didn't expect to see you here." I turned.

"Well, to be honest, I wasn't expecting to be here myself. Simon, nice to see you. How are you?"

He was wearing a badge and one of those aprons with a zipped pocket for change on. He had a pot plant in each arm, and appeared to be making his way towards a stall nearby.

"Oh, I'm ok." He put the plants down at the stall and then returned to greet me properly. Unexpectedly he touched my arm. "You look better than you did too."

"Ha, thanks. I guess it couldn't get worse."

"True." He smiled kindly.

"So are you involved in organising this?"

"Yep, for my sins. I'm a member of the congregation here, and we're setting up a food bank and charitable fund for people who fall on hard times in the local area."

"Sounds interesting."

"Yeah, well, we wanted to do more than just provide people with food. I mean, it's great that so many organisations are doing that now, it's a vital resource. But we feel like we can do more. Our aim is to set up a community hub where people can come for training, advice, support and maybe even financial grants for specific projects."

I smiled. "What a great project. Sounds fascinating."

"Don't show too much enthusiasm, we might end up roping you in."

I laughed. "Well if there is one thing I have on my hands right now, it's time. I'm still working out what I'm going to do career wise, and I'm fortunate enough not to be in a rush, so if you want me, I am at your disposal."

"Really?" His eyebrows were raised, and his cheeks showed the hint of a smile.

"Really."

"Well, tomorrow afternoon we're opening the hall up for the weekly food bank. Then after that we're meeting to talk about how we will make our plan work to turn it into something even bigger and better. Would you like to come?"

"Sure. For the meeting? Or for the food bank too?"

"Well, if you've got the time, an extra pair of hands putting together the food packages would be fabulous. Then you'll have earned your place at the meeting." He looked satisfied with his recruitment approach.

"Deal. Look, here's my new number, text me through the details later."

"I will, better go now though, the marigolds are getting a bit of interest, so I should go and pay attention to the customers." I watched as Simon seamlessly struck up conversation with an elderly couple admiring his wares.

After a look around the stalls, I went for a cup of tea in a café and read the paper. It felt good to have something in my diary before seeing Sara. It was a buffer. The news was full of the potential leadership challenge I had read about previously. It seemed as though a vote of no confidence in the leader of the party might be imminent. While he had been popular with grass roots supporters, he had failed to make his mark in Westminster, slowly losing the support of his MPs. I would be interested to hear Sara's thoughts on it, although I wasn't sure where the conversation would take us. I could imagine her at the dispatch box opposite the prime minister. Her piercing wit and intelligence would be wounding to a political opponent. It made me smile to think of her marching into Downing Street one day in her Paul Smith suit, calling everyone darling.

The church hall looked very different when I returned the following afternoon. One side of the room was a mass of carrier bags containing an eclectic mix of food and produce. A small team of volunteers was sorting through the melee, filling boxes with selections that would sustain a family for a few days. It made me sad to think that there were people within walking distance for whom this was fundamentally how they ensured their children ate. Simon noticed me after a moment, and beckoned me over.

"OK," he said, gesturing to the carrier bags, "can you separate out all the rice and pasta from the rest of the food there first? Then, once you've done that, ensure that each box has at least one or both of those things in."

I nodded and walked into the buzz.

"Thanks, Cameron, I really appreciate your help."

"You're welcome. I should be thanking you really, it was only a few days ago I was talking about doing something a bit more connected to where I live, and here I am." He nodded and smiled, and got on with organising the rest of the volunteers.

It wasn't long before each box had a good balanced mix of produce in. "Well done, Cameron, you're a quick worker," said Simon. I blushed at the simple compliment. "And it's a good thing too. Look." He gestured out of the window. A queue of people had formed, waiting outside the locked front door. I looked at the faces, which didn't match the Oliver Twist idea I had originally had of who might be coming. They weren't all pale, skinny and in rags, they were mums with children mostly, with deep frown lines in their foreheads. There were men too, most without children, young and old, big and small. It was a sad little line.

"Ok everyone," said Simon, once he'd checked the boxes, "are we ready? Remember, this isn't just about food, this is about support. Smile!" Everyone readied their grins as he made for the big double doors and pulled back the bolt.

People filed in quickly in and filled the hall with chatter. Children could be seen poking their fingers into different boxes, being told by their mums not to touch. I stood with the other volunteers behind the long table laden with boxes. A woman wearing a hijab, with her head down approached me. Once she was close enough I saw she had a small smile. I treated her to the best welcoming face I could. She had a baby in one arm, and two toddlers holding onto her clothing. Her movements were cautious.

"How are you today?" I asked quietly. For the first time, she looked up at me.

"Fine thank you. These three are keeping me busy."

"I bet they do. Hang on, don't go for that box, there's another one here that I think will suit you better." I pointed at the one I had selected – it had a Cbeebies magazine in it from a few weeks back.

She beamed at me. I carried the box over to the pushchair she had come in with. "He only likes being carried at the moment," she said, her eyes on her baby son. "He'll have to go back in the buggy now though, else I'll never get this lot home." He mewed as she put him into his seat and scrunched up his face in the way that only small babies do. The other two boys took the opportunity to run into the far corner of the hall. She frowned and called their names, but they appeared oblivious.

"Don't worry," I said, "let me keep an eye on this one while you go and get them." While she was gathering together her two tearaways, I managed to jam the box of food into the basket underneath the pushchair.

"Thank you," she said, when she returned with the boys, who looked grumpy at being removed from the ancient dusty radiator which had been fascinating them so much.

"Well, I hope you have a good evening." She smiled and nodded, put her head down, and was quickly gone.

After an hour, most of the boxes had gone, and the crowd had dwindled. "Fancy a cuppa?" asked Simon.

"Oh yes please," I said, my face aching with all the smiling and being polite to strangers.

"Biscuits?"

"Of course."

The time came to close up and lock the doors. There was very little food left, and the room looked stark, with only empty carrier bags and a couple of boxes remaining in the now empty hall. It didn't take long to tidy up, and soon I was shown into a small room off the main hall for the meeting.

More tea was served, this time from a large utilitarian metal teapot into institutional green crockery. It was a long way from frothy lattes served in tall glasses in Holborn. It was comforting and real.

Simon started the meeting, and it quickly became apparent he was the driving force behind all of these activities. He started by thanking everyone for their help with the food bank, and agreeing arrangements for the following week. Then, he moved us on. He rested his elbows on the table in front of him and made a steeple with his fingers. He paused, before speaking.

"I want us to do more than just feed these people. Think of the men, women and children you saw today. Hunger isn't their problem; poverty is. And the solution is not to simply give them money, it isn't sustainable. What we need is to offer these people a way out of the situation they are in. What is it that we, as a community, can offer them?" He left the question hanging for a moment before continuing. "I think we have a lot to offer, Jan," he gestured towards a woman in her 60s with silver hair, "your cake baking is legendary. But are there skills you could teach some of these people about day to day living – shopping, cooking, making a budget stretch?"

Jan nodded. "I raised four children on a pittance. I'm better off now than I was back in the 60s and 70s. I learnt it all from my mum."

"Exactly," said Simon, "but I wonder whether we can help pass on your mum's skills? I'm not sure all of the people we see here will have had that experience."

"Yes," said a man in his forties, wearing a yellow T shirt and sporting tousled hair that probably hadn't been combed, "I'd be happy to take some people down to the allotment and talk about growing veg and stuff."

Simon spoke again. "Great, and we could run CV workshops and get companies in who are recruiting to support people who want to get back into work."

I raised my hand slightly, and Simon nodded towards me. "I hate to say it, but aren't we the wrong people to be deciding this? Shouldn't we be asking them?" Raised eyebrows from around the table pointed in my direction. "I know that you know them all far better than I do. But what I do know is how disempowering poverty is. And here we are, a group of people who don't need the support of a food bank, most of us with decent jobs and incomes, deciding how best we will help those less fortunate than ourselves. I think the ideas all sound great, but perhaps we should ask the people themselves what they want?"

There was a silence. "You know," said Jan, "I hadn't even thought of that. We should ask them."

"Yes," said Simon, with a small smile, "we should. What about next week, Cameron? Would you be able to help us to talk to people while they're picking up their food about what we could do to support them more?"

"Er, well, yes, I suppose I can do that." I was surprised at the willingness of the group to hand over the control of this to me. "I'll need your help though."

"Of course," said Simon, and the yellow T shirt man nodded his agreement. We spent the next hour planning the questions we would ask and how everything would work at the next food bank event. By the time the meeting was finished we had planned that the session would not only involve the usual food boxes, but there would be an opportunity for people to sit down, have a drink and a snack and talk to one of us about what they thought we could do to make things better for the community. I left the church hall with a bubble of excitement inside me that carried me home to my flat. I cooked myself a simple dinner of jacket potato and beans, and found a film on Netflix to entertain me for the evening.

Chapter 20

The train to London reminded me of my old job, and the routine I used to have of reading research on my prospects on the way. No prospects this time, just me, Sara and a big city. I wasn't wearing my usual business attire either, I had opted instead for smart jeans and a simple white shirt with small blue flowers on. It was a favourite, and it gave me confidence. I had even put on the eye liner that I generally only wore for work or dates. I knew this wasn't a date though, and even as I put it on I berated myself. The landscape swept by and my eyes were caught by the overhead cables running in uneven parallel, moving in and out as the train sped on. I balled my hands into fists. I needed to stay strong. It was her who had cut the ties. Not me. I needed to stop acting like I was trying to win her back. If anything, it should be the other way round. Somehow, I couldn't bring myself to be angry though. I just felt sad.

On arrival into Marylebone I put my headphones in and walked down the long platform to the outside world to the strains of music that would ordinarily have been too loud for me. I walked to Edgware Road and descended into the depths of the city via escalator.

I was 45 minutes early. I walked down the swanky Whitehall street, and looked up at the windows, working out which one was Sara's. It was odd to be back here. I walked back towards the Thames, bought myself a cup of tea in a paper cup, and sat on a bench watching the muddy water flow by. The faint smell of the sea was ever present, along with petrol fumes and the general odour of London that was somehow unique to this city. It was good to be back. Boats passed, suited men and women hurried along the pavement, and aeroplanes soared overhead. The tea helped strengthen my resolve before I started the short walk back to the grand entrance that heralded Sara's apartment building. I was just walking up the steps, when I heard a voice from behind me.

"Cameron." I turned. There she was. Luminous.

"Oh, hi. I was expecting to see you upstairs." I berated myself for such an asinine comment and went red.

"Yes. I just popped out for some flowers." Sara's arm was full of yellow, violet and white blooms.

"Very Mrs Dalloway," I said.

"Well, if I don't buy them for myself, who will?" She gave an absent minded smile while I wondered how to respond. "Come on then, let's go up and sit down." I smiled, and we walked in and took the stairs to her domain. We walked into her apartment and I immediately wished that we had agreed to meet somewhere else. Coming back to the place of our first meeting, our first kiss, felt like pulling a plaster from a wound too quickly. "Take a seat. I'll pop these in water and get us some coffees. I assume you'll have one?" I nodded and she disappeared.

Shadows of her cupping my hands emerged unbidden, the sigh she'd given as I undid the buttons on her blouse one by one. I recalled her scent as I kissed her neck, and the thrill of her pulling my top up and over my head, throwing it onto the floor without looking back. I made a small noise in the back of my throat, which brought me back into the here and now and the next step we were about to take. I wasn't sure where we were headed, but the outcome of today was likely to be different to that day months ago.

Sara walked back in, her red shoes reflecting the sun coming in through the window. She sat across the low lounge table from me. "So," she said, as though opening a meeting. The word hung there for a moment. "I had a plan of all the things I was going to say to you, Cam, but now you're here, I just don't know."

I felt my face heat up. "I know. It's odd isn't it." I put my mug to my lips, but removed it again. It was too hot to drink. I replaced it on its elegant coaster.

"You got my letter though?"

"Yes. My phone broke."

"That will explain why you didn't return my calls. Perhaps." Sara twiddled with a ring on her little finger and then took a deep breath. "I'm so sorry, Cameron. It was just such an extreme turn of events. I've never been subject to that kind of scrutiny in my life. And yes, I know, nor have you. And the party took over. They told me I should distance myself from you, make sure not to give anyone any further ammunition." She picked up her mug and took a small sip. "After that call we shared, I felt wretched. By the next day I knew I'd made a mistake. More than that though, I knew I'd done the worst possible thing. I'd abandoned you."

Tears started to fall down my face unbidden. Hearing her admit her part in all of this was more of a relief than I expected. She walked around the table and sat next to me, taking my hand. The warmth of her touch was the final straw and I sobbed. She took me into her arms as I cried. There was nothing I could do.

There we sat for what seemed like hours. She soothingly stroked my back, and whispered reassuring things in my ear.

"God," I said after a while, "I'm such a snotty soggy mess."

"Yes, darling, you are. But it's ok. I won't tell." We both laughed. She found me a handkerchief infused with her own perfume. I dabbed at my eyes, cursing the eye liner I'd put on earlier in the day. I blew my nose, and picked up my coffee once again, which was now tepid. My mouth was dry from all the crying, so I gulped it down hungrily. "Cameron," said Sara quietly, "can you ever forgive me?"

"Of course."

"But I mean, I know that one can never go back. But do you think you could love me again?" Her words dangled in front of my face and I felt myself go cold. I hadn't expected this. "I know that it might take time, that it wouldn't go back to normal overnight. It's just, I love you, Cam. I've not stopped thinking about you. I'd started to believe that I would never hear from you again. I called so many times. I even came to your apartment once, but you were out. I wrote and for so long I heard nothing. For a time I was worried. And then," she sighed, "then I decided that you had decided you didn't want to be found."

"I guess I didn't for a while," I said, my head down, for the first time feeling the edges of regret for what I'd done with Hayley in Ibiza. "I do love you, Sara," I said quietly, surprising myself with my candidness. If today had taught me nothing, it had taught me that.

"Oh darling, thank God," Sara pulled me in for a kiss, but I pulled back. She furrowed her brow and waited for me to speak.

"I'm not sure it's going to be that simple though. There are things I need to tell you about. So much has happened since we last saw each other."

Sara's eyes clouded over, and I saw a tear forming. I couldn't bear to hurt her, but I knew we couldn't just pick up where we left off.

"I didn't think that you would ever want to see me again. Even when I read your letter, I thought this was about closure. I suppose I was protecting myself," I said, holding Sara's hand and stroking it gently. She nodded, but didn't speak. "And I'm not saying I don't want to be with you."

"What are you saying then?" It was a reasonable question.

"Things got really bad after we spoke that day. Even Tom and I fell out. I was completely alone. No job, no girlfriend, no friend. The media were camped outside my apartment and I had no idea what I was going to do. I was in a dark place." Sara nodded gravely. She knew there was more.

"And then?"

"And then someone rescued me. That makes it all sound rather melodramatic doesn't it? But it's true. I was rescued. Within 24 hours I was in another country with someone who cared about me and listened to me. It was uncomplicated and what I needed. What I thought I needed." Sara pressed her lips together and withdrew her hand.

"Who?"

"Hayley."

"Your ex?"

"Yes." We both sat in silence for a few moments.

"Did you..." her voice trailed off, and she began to cry. I'd never seen her this vulnerable before and all I wanted to do was put my arms around her and tell her it would all be ok. I knew I couldn't. It wouldn't be fair.

"Yes." A noise that was somewhere between a sob and a laugh came from her mouth. "I'm sorry, Sara. I'm so very very sorry."

"You really had that little faith in me that you thought I would never come back to you? You just gave up?" She didn't sound angry, just sad.

"Perhaps I did. But what else was I to think? At the most extraordinary moment of my life to date everything I relied upon was gone."

She wiped her eyes and looked at me. "Are you with her now?"

I shook my head vigorously. "No, no."

"But you were." She exhaled. "You were right when you said it wasn't simple. You've moved on."

"No, I haven't. I just had to do something. I'm sorry. There's nothing I can say, I know that." I clasped my hands together. "It didn't even feel like reality. I had been taken away into some kind of parallel universe." Sara looked up at me and I immediately regretted my choice of words.

"Everything has changed now hasn't it?"

"Yes. I wish it hadn't. But yes, it has." I wanted to say that the reason I had needed to get so far away and so irrefutably draw a line under me and Sara, was down to how much she meant to me. I swallowed the words because I knew that they wouldn't make her feel any better.

"You know, I really thought when you got in touch that you might be able to forgive me and we could start again." She looked to the sky, and sighed. "I was wrong."

I bit my lip, trying to stop the tears that threatened to come. It really was over. There was no going back.

"I should go," I said after a few moments silence. There was nothing more to say. Sara said nothing, she just stared ahead. I wanted to hold her, to shout at her, shake away all the mistakes we'd made and make us both forget. I'd never seen her this way before, and I knew instinctively that the last thing she would want was for me to stay. She nodded very slightly. I started to gather my possessions, clutching my bag to me as tightly as my emotions. Now was not a time for me to have another breakdown.

With each step I took away from her, towards the front door, I wanted to turn and throw myself before her and plead for us to try again, no matter how hopeless. It wasn't out of any respect for myself that I didn't, but respect for her. I left with as much dignity as I could gather, gently closing her door behind me. The latch dropped in time with the first of another avalanche of my tears.

I walked down to the river. I didn't care that I looked a sobbing emotional mess. The anonymity of London meant that, much to my relief, no one stopped me. I returned to the bench I had sat on before. It wasn't that it was over – I had always believed that to be the case – it was that we had actually had a chance and I had ruined it. I watched flotsam and jetsam meander down the Thames, wishing I could go with it, away from this place, this day, this situation.

I don't recall much about the journey home. I just know that I made it. I thought about calling Tom, but decided against it. There was nothing anyone could do for me now. I found a bottle of gin in the cupboard and poured myself a liberal slug. I downed it and poured another. I put the stereo on and the strains of a song I had loved as a teenager slid from the radio. At once I was taken back to my youth, to Caroline, to the crimes I almost committed and the fatal end to our love. More gin, louder music. I stood in the middle of the room, swaying, eyes closed, transported into an alcohol infused version of my history. The words of passion, anger and grief of those now sepia days flooded my being and the air that surrounded me. I was lost to the present, searching through old diaries, finding CDs that took me back to an age that was long gone, lamenting a person who no longer was. It was too much to contain, and the shopping list pad that usually sat on my fridge was liberated and became a receptacle for the words I could no longer hold onto. Random phrases, words, scenes from my life. I replayed the moments that had cut me and left me wounded, but the moment I had replayed them, somehow they felt less real. I wasn't sure they had ever really happened. More gin, more music and the room spun and I swayed. Each page I filled was torn away and discarded, and a new one begun.

Chapter 21

I awoke with a start in a heap on the sofa, covered in crumpled pieces of illegible paper. The sun was beginning to rise and the clock showed 5am. My head ached in a way it hadn't in years, and my mouth felt as though it had rotted away in the intervening hours. I lifted my head, and the room tilted dramatically. I staggered to the bathroom to be sick.

I caught myself in the mirror. I looked a wreck. My face was a pale shade of grey and my lips almost transparent. I was glad there was no one to see me in such a state.

Returning to the living room, I swept the papers to the floor and switched on the TV. I sipped at a glass of tepid water, which was a struggle. Mindless daytime television filled the room, providing a welcome distraction.

The following days and weeks passed in a blur of misery and regret. The only bright spot was my weekly volunteering at the food bank. It was the only place where I felt like I was giving anything of any value. It was the only place I felt like I was of any value at all. Simon always asked how I was, and what was going on in my life, but I deflected, not wanting him to know how empty my life had become. I continued to attend planning meetings. There was a glimmer of hope that we could get the funding for a community hub, and soon I found myself embroiled in writing a detailed funding application to a charitable trust for such a resource. It was a welcome focus.

"I think we stand a good chance," said Simon, sitting in my flat, as we pored over the application and gave it one final proof read before submitting it.

"I hope so," I said, "we've done everything we can."

"That's generous of you, Cam, but you know as well as I do that you wrote this application and masterminded the whole idea. It was you who found the opportunity." He paused, and sipped the weak and milky instant coffee on the table between us. "I know this hasn't been a happy time for you." I started to speak, but he waved his hand. "No need to say anything. Some things are clear without words, and I have no intention of prying into your affairs. I just want you to know that if this succeeds, it will be down to you." I smiled, grateful for our growing friendship.

"So," I said. "Shall we?" My hand hovered over the 'submit' button. He gave me a warm smile.

"Go for it, Cam."

I pressed down on the button, and the application vanished from view into an online portal, to reappear in front of a committee of Trustees at a meeting the following week.

"Cheers," said Simon, holding his mug up. I clinked it with my cup of strong tea and we both heaved a sigh of relief. "So what now?"

"No idea. I'm keeping my eyes open for work opportunities, but nothing appeals. I suppose I'm in a luxurious position really, I still have a month of pay left. I really should count my blessings when I look at the alternative. Some of the people we help really don't have more than a fiver in the bank to last until the end of the month, do they? I'm not sure what right I have to be so picky."

"Don't feel guilty for what you have. Would those people be in a better position if you were in the same situation as them? No. It is because of your relative comfort that you have been able to do something good."

"You're right, it really is a privileged position isn't it?" I sighed. "Refill?"

"No thanks. I've got a better idea." Simon grinned, and pulled a tiny bottle of prosecco from his bag. "I thought we ought to celebrate."

"Perfect. I'll fetch some glasses." It was the first drink I'd had since that awful night and it was good to be celebrating.

There was only really enough for a modest glass each, but the bubbles and the simple pleasure of finishing something was enough to relax us both.

"How are things for you now?" asked Simon during a lull in conversation. We'd been seeing each other regularly for the last few weeks. This wasn't about my general well-being.

"That's very diplomatic." I smiled.

"You don't have to tell me anything you don't want to. I just wasn't sure if there was anyone you were talking to at the moment." He drained his glass. "Perhaps I'm prying, but you seem happier this evening than you have for a while. That's good to see."

"Thanks. I think it's safe to say that I've had less 'colourful' episodes in my life than the last few weeks. If this is your way of asking about Sara…"

"No, no, of course not, that's your business," he waved his hand apologetically as he spoke.

"There's not much to tell to be honest, and it's quite nice to share. We're not together any more. I think it's safe to say that having a crowd of photographers on your doorstep and the red tops stalking every move you make is not good for a fledgling relationship." I sighed. "There was a moment when I thought things might work out, but, well, it wasn't to be."

"She's a fool to let you go."

"I wouldn't be too sympathetic. Let's just say that to a certain extent I dug my own grave there. I shan't bore you with the details."

"You're welcome to bore me. But whatever it is, don't be too hard on yourself. You've had a hell of a time, and I think you've managed to come out of it with real dignity."

I laughed. "That's got to be the first time this situation has been described as anything approaching dignified. Thank you though. And thanks for getting me involved with the food bank, and the community hub bid. It has made all the difference, given me a purpose I'm not sure I would have had otherwise."

"It was purely selfish. You're good at this stuff."

"Well, here's to this stuff!"

"This stuff!" we clinked our now empty glasses together and laughed again. There was something simple and easy about his company. He was the kind of guy I used to go out on dates with when I was in my late teens. No stress, no pressure, no tension. No sexual attraction.

"Thanks for being my friend. Oh God, I'm not even drunk." I laughed at myself. "I'll be declaring undying love next. Seriously though. Thank you."

"My pleasure."

Chapter 22

It had been a while since Tom and I had met for a gin and tonic. I drummed my fingers on the bar, not sure why heart was pounding. When his face appeared and he smiled I felt myself relax.

"So, darling, do you have a plan?" he asked.

"Well, I've been checking all the job sites and the local paper and stuff but there's nothing there really that seems to float my boat." He held up his hand to stop me.

"Oh bugger work, Cam, I mean your love life. Do you have a plan? You've been nursing your broken heart for too long now. We need to get you back out there."

"Out where? I'm not a hooker."

"Oh ha ha, very funny, sweetie. Now don't be obtuse." He peered down his nose at me like a school ma'am. "I know it's been grim. But with your brooding good looks and the troubled look in your eyes, women won't be able to resist you."

I sighed. "Really? God I'm not sure I have the energy for all that lark."

Tom threw a hand to his brow, and spoke in mock horror. "Nurse, the screens, it's worse than I thought. Next thing I know you'll be sharing your meals with your four cats and exclusively wearing knitwear."

"That'll never happen. For one, I'm allergic to cats."

"Oh be quiet! It's decided, we're setting you up a profile. Look – I started it earlier, it was a slow afternoon at work."

He wafted his phone in front of me and I took it from him for a closer look.

"Started it? This has all information bar my inside leg measurement on it already! It's lucky Damien didn't catch you. Interested in DIY and car maintenance? What? Do you even know me?"

"I have used creative license. All the girls love a handy woman."

"You make it sound like I have a tool belt on at all times. I put up a shelf once, and occasionally put up Ikea furniture, but that's about it."

"Spoil sport. Ok then, what shall we write?"

"Hell, I don't know. I need another drink if you're going to make me do this."

"It's a deal." Tom turned to the barman who had been pretending not to giggle at our conversation. "Two more G and Ts please love."

I got home bleary but happy and fell into bed. I had no real intention of jumping back into the dating pool, such as it was. But it had been a good night of the sort we used to have, before all the drama.

I woke up feeling unexpectedly clear-headed and happy. I checked my phone. It was already after 10.30am and there were a couple of messages waiting for me. The first was from Tom.

//I hope you've logged into your profile. I took the liberty of checking in for you first thing. You've already had some bites… Mwah darling xxx//

I laughed out loud. He was incorrigible, but he was in the most part good for me. The next message was from Simon.

//Cam, are you about this morning? I've got news and want to tell you in person. Dante's at 11am for coffee and croissants?//

I pulled up a message to reply to Simon.

//Just waking up. Will throw myself into the shower and head over x//

"Gosh," I said, when I saw Simon sitting at the bistro table in the café, two steaming mugs of coffee and a large plate of croissants at the ready. He was already tucking into one with gusto. "Are we having a party?"

He stood up. "Well we should, Cam. I just heard. We got the funding."

I froze. "All of it?"

"All of it!"

I screamed, and without thinking hurled myself into his arms. We hugged for a few seconds, until we both felt a bit awkward.

"Oh, Simon, this is amazing." We sat down and I took a slurp of coffee and helped myself to a pain au chocolat. "I am so excited. Where do we start?"

"Well, that's why I want to talk to you. The first thing we need to do is employ a director of the hub; someone to lead it from the start and really get everything going. Volunteers are great, but this needs full time dedication from someone who knows their stuff."

"Oh now, that is an exciting thought. I've definitely got some thoughts based on people I've worked with before." I started running through my mental set of Rolodex. Working at the university had put me in touch with no end of interesting people and I was sure there would be people who would be thrilled to take up this kind of position.

"I don't think you are understanding me," said Simon, dabbing his mouth with a red napkin. "I'm saying that I've spoken to everyone involved, and we're all agreed. We want you to do it."

"What? Me? Are you sure?" I put down my half eaten pastry and then picked it back up again. I didn't know what to do with my hands. "But I have no experience. I've never done anything like this before."

"But you have. You've devoted so much of your own time to the food bank. And while you've maybe not done exactly this before, it's obvious that you've got the skills. I mean, we're not going to be able to pay you what you would get at the uni."

"No, don't worry about that. I just wonder whether it's a good idea. You saw what happened before. I would hate for all that stuff in the papers to come back and haunt the organisation. I don't want to be a liability." My words came out in a rush.

"It's a risk worth taking. Don't forget I know what happened, and now Sara's off the scene, I really can't see it all coming back again." I felt my heart drop a little at the mention of her name. "You're good, Cam, you have so much to offer. Let's just do this."

We sat, ate, drank and talked some more. Mid-morning pastries became lunch, and by mid-afternoon I appeared to have a new job. I walked back to my apartment in a daze, replaying what had just happened. I had been given an unbelievable opportunity, and blank canvas on which to work. Simon was right, it was less than I had been paid before, but it was enough. It was a chance to start again and do something new.

Chapter 23

My new office was little more than a broom cupboard. A desk, which filled approximately a third of the room, meant that in order to let anyone in to speak to me, I had to wheel my dog eared chair away from the door. Our budget had stretched to a new computer, which was great, although the wifi was somewhat flaky. I wrote a note and pinned it to the cork pin board above the desk reminding me to find the church hall's router, and see if it needed to be moved.

The early days flew by in a whirlwind of getting bank accounts set up, putting together a meaningful plan, beyond the wish list that we had applied for, and working out how we were going to make it all happen. It was good to be fully engaged in work once again, although this was very different to what I'd done before. I found myself waking up in a good mood, and then walking with the proverbial spring in my step to my poky office. There were no high security swipe cards for me, just a couple of heavy duty keys that jangled in my bag with each step I took. I was often the first person to arrive at the hall each day, but around mid-morning I would hear the sounds of the hall being set up, whether for a stay and play session for local parents and toddlers, or for a knitting circle, or for a meeting of some description. I grew used to the sound of the urn being switched on, the old boiler noisily heating water for the inevitable washing up and the chatter of busy voices. It became my backdrop, and stopped me from feeling isolated. While we had plenty of volunteers to help with the set-up of the hub, there was a lot of time when it was just me in my little office, working out what to do next. The radio was my other saviour. I had never really been one for Radio 4, but somehow in this new profession, it felt appropriate. I often found myself taking in Women's Hour by osmosis as I contacted suppliers, set up partnerships and added yet more tasks to the 'to-do' list.

I was drinking a cup of tea while trying to establish what we needed to do in terms of publicity, when I heard a familiar voice on the magazine programme that had just begun.

"Thank you. That was Sara Lorenzo, MP for Mallington South. Welcome, Sara, it's good to have you here. What have we taken you away from this morning?" said the respectable, if slightly plummy journalist Harriet Barnes.

"I've just finished a surgery in my constituency, which was, as always, fascinating. One of the real perks of my job is meeting so many people."

"What sort of issues have you come up against today?"

"Oh all sorts really. There's been some really passionate conversations in recent months about the introduction of wheelie bins in part of the constituency. It really does seem to divide neighbourhoods." I could hear the smile in her voice as she spoke.

"What's your role in that kind of situation?"

"Well, naturally, that is a council decision, and I wouldn't ordinarily meddle in councillors' affairs – they are of course democratically elected too, and, one would hope, acting in their communities' best interests. For now, I am listening to all the views, and will be watching closely to see how the new system works." She took a breath in. "I have also been hearing a lot from people who feel really strongly about the health bill the government has put forward."

"Yes," said the presenter, "as Shadow Health Secretary you will presumably be playing a key role in opposing such a bill?"

"Absolutely. I think the concept of moving to a system where people need to pay for GP appointments is completely at odds with the spirit of the NHS – the National Health Service – as it was set up. I cannot, in all clear conscience, support a bill that means that the most deprived in our communities – who by the way, are also those who are most likely to be unwell – are penalised for needing medical help. Perhaps £10 for me is acceptable, but what if that's the difference between your family eating or not eating for a few days?" Sara let the question hang.

"It is interesting you bring up your own financial position, because you are a well-documented 'champagne socialist', if you'll pardon the phrase, aren't you?"

Sara's immediate good natured laugh trickled into my ears, and I found myself smiling involuntarily.

"I suppose so. Personally though, I really don't think it matters where you come from. Take my opposite number, Arnold Danvers, the Health Secretary. He is, rightly, not judged for his northern, working class roots. He has risen to a respected and powerful position in Government. I may not agree with him, but few can deny his importance in the UK. By the same token, one would hope that the fact that I was privately educated and from a wealthy family should not be a stick with which to beat me. Yes, roots are important. But it really is all about what you do in the here and now, not where you have come from."

"Well put," said Harriet Barnes. "Following on from that though, if people are able to judge you for what you do, what do you think the public made of some very lurid stories about you in the tabloid press a few months ago?"

I heard what sounded like a sigh from Sara before she spoke. My hand hovered over the radio's off switch. I wasn't sure I wanted to hear this. I couldn't bring myself to though, so like a horror film viewer watching from behind a cushion, I continued to listen.

"Well, I think it is very easy for people looking for a salacious story to turn what was perhaps an error in judgement into something much more sordid. As you know, the investigation that followed exonerated me, so I am keen to move on and focus on more serious matters."

"But do you think the public are ready to do that?"

"I can't speak for them. I can however vouch for those I've seen in recent weeks in my own constituency. The vast majority of them are far more interested in talking about the inequalities that some of my constituents will face if this health bill goes through. My job is to represent their views in parliament."

"Do you feel there is more scrutiny of you as an openly gay MP?" Harriet wasn't letting it go.

"No, not really. It's right that I am accountable to the public for my actions. That has little bearing on who I have relationships with. In the most part, I really don't think people give a damn about who I have dinner with on a Friday night."

Harriet giggled. "That's fair enough. But is there a personal cost to all this? In the stories that followed the claims that were made relating to the donation you made to your former college, you were very clear that the relationship you were having with a member of staff was very separate to any financial decisions you were making."

"Correct." I thought I could detect some frostiness in her voice.

"Are you still together?"

There was a pause. I held my breath, even though I knew the answer.

"No. Political life isn't always compatible with a successful private life, especially with the additional pressures of the media."

"Thank you, Sara Lorenzo, Shadow Health Secretary. We'll be back after the news with more on the new health bill and recent spats in the House of Commons over migrant workers." The pips sounded, I switched off the radio and exhaled. I'm fairly sure I had breathed throughout the rest of the interview, but the respite the news gave was welcome. I went to the kitchen to make myself some more tea. I was, unaccountably, hurt by the fact she hadn't mentioned my name, or said anything specific about me. Of course she didn't. There were many hundreds of thousands of people listening, and she wouldn't go into her private life beyond where she had already gone. She just sounded so poised, so level, so unflappable. She was a million miles away from the woman I had last spent time with a few weeks ago. Of course, that was to be expected. It was all my fault, I had hurt her, she had moved on. She had a job to do. She wasn't going to weep live on air to the British public and beg me to come back. And, if I was honest, I wouldn't want her to. I was still standing motionless in the kitchen a few minutes later. This wouldn't do. I'd been in the office for several hours with no break, so I picked up my wallet and headed down the road for a walk. I treated myself to a coffee in a cafe a few streets away and scrolled through my Twitter time-line on my phone. I wasn't the only one who had been listening to the interview by the looks of things. The health bill was polarising views, although the majority of people on my feed were against plans to start charging people to see their doctor. It reminded me of an article I read recently about social media being an echo chamber – lulling you into thinking that the majority of people share the same view as you, because you can block or unfollow anyone who disagrees. One Tweet did catch my eye though.

//Great handling of Barnes by Lorenzo there, although if the rumours are true, it was Barnes who was dining with her last Friday night...//

I read it again. Surely there was no truth in that was there? There had been rumours about Harriet Barnes through the years, but she had never confirmed or denied them. It was her prerogative of course, but my stomach lurched when I replayed in my head that giggle she had offered up when Sara talked about dining out. I shuddered. Of course, a woman like Sara would move on. I was moving on too in some parts of my life. I had no choice.

My phone bleeped. I noticed the dating app for the first time since Tom had set it up. Maybe he was right. Maybe it was time to get my feet wet again. I opened it up and spotted a couple of messages. I was surprised that people had already responded. One was clearly from someone looking for a no strings hook-up. Not really for me. I sent back a polite but tepid response. Next was a cautious hello from someone who was as new to this as I was.

//Hi, not sure of the etiquette of this really, but I read your profile, and you seem nice. So, hi :) Pip//

I tapped through to her profile. It was hard to see what her face was like from her photo, hidden as it was underneath a cute mustard woolly hat. There was a quiet smile under there though. I grinned to myself and started to tap out a response.

//Hi, I'm a newbie too, so don't worry. Nice hat. Cam //

The radio interview acted as a hard line written in ink under our relationship, and I renewed my moving on efforts. Things moved forward apace with the hub, thanks to the dedication of the volunteers. We were already beginning to grow the service, opening the food bank three times a week instead of just once. The next step was to start bringing in other sorts of support for the people that we began to call clients. To start with it was just me, with a little desk in the hall, helping people go through the benefit claims and giving advice on budget management. It was a steep learning curve. I had the good fortune of never having needed to claim benefits myself, and I was amazed at the dizzying list of pieces of evidence and reference numbers and so much information that needed to be provided even to be considered for any benefit. The forms were long, bureaucratic and laborious. In the early days, I spent time online trying to ascertain the best approach to take when supporting people. I also did my fair share of reading job application forms, correcting spelling mistakes, and encouraging people, women in particular, to talk about their skills in running a home, in terms that related to the jobs they were applying for.

Chapter 24

It was a couple of months later, when I had employed two part time staff to work a few hours every day to take on the advising, and a local cafe had offered to run a subsidised mini-cafe, that I stood in the hall, looking around me. What hit me most were the smiling faces, the people who used to scurry in for food, and then scurry back out again, heads down, now sitting with a cup of inexpensive tea and a biscuit, chatting to one another. We'd been able to invest in play equipment for a small area dedicated to the many children who came in with their parents. Somehow, on a small budget, we had really started to make a difference. We still ran a food bank, but increasingly, we were seeing people coming back to tell us that they had succeeded in getting a job, or perhaps they had managed to get their electricity reconnected. It was heartening to know that the vision that Simon and our colleagues had had was already being realised.

I had fallen into a routine at home too. I met Tom once a week for gossip and drinks in a bar in town, and Simon and I tended to go for an early evening curry on a Friday night. My life had become remarkably uncomplicated. There had been a few further messages with Pip in the hat on the dating app, but somewhere along the line, it had petered out. I wasn't particularly bothered. My time was largely taken up with the community hub. There was still so much more to do. The more services we offered, the more people came through our doors.

All political coverage on TV was about the controversial health bill that Sara had spoken so vehemently against. Spending time with the people at the hub had made me realised she was right. If she was a champagne socialist, then perhaps I was a gin socialist. People had taken to the streets to protest the bill, but given the majority the Government had, it looked likely that the bill would go through. Sara could be seen most weeks speaking to political rallies, and beseeching MPs 'with a conscience' to vote the bill down.

On the night of the vote, journalists were reporting that there was a chance, albeit slim, that the Government would lose. I headed into the night to meet Tom hopeful that perhaps good would win out this once.

"How are you doing darling?" asked Tom over the table full of Chinese food we were stuffing ourselves with. "You've been so busy lately, but you seem much happier after all that happened."

"I guess I've moved on. You can't stay still forever. The hub takes up so much of my energy, and it's great seeing it beginning to make a difference to people."

"Well good for you darling. You deserve it. You don't need an analyst do you?"

"Ha! I wish I could afford you sweetie. Will you pass over the chow mein? Yeah, I do miss your research skills. Sadly I have to do all my own research these days. There is something nice about that though. At the college I was always a tiny cog in a massive machine. Now I'm..."

"The machine?"

I laughed. "Well no, but perhaps the head gasket?"

"See, I said you were good at fixing cars!" Tom took a triumphant swig of his drink. "And on that note, any love life interest?"

"No, not lately. To be honest, I'm not sure I've got the time for all that right now."

"Boring," said Tom in a sing song voice while simultaneously rolling his eyes. I shrugged. There wasn't much more to say really. I felt a finger tap my shoulder.

"Hi – are you Cam?" I turned and looked at a young woman looking down at me quizzically. She looked familiar, but I couldn't place her.

"Um, yes," I said, desperately trying to work out where I'd seen her before.

She smiled ruefully. "Perhaps I should put my hat back on?"

"Pip!" I said suddenly, "of course. You look different in real life."

Pip laughed. "So do you. Look, I won't disturb your meal, but do come over and say hi if you get a moment." She gestured towards a table with a group of people who looked like they were celebrating a birthday. She smiled, revealing dimples in her cheeks, and skipped back over to where her friends were.

Tom raised an eyebrow. "So much for not having time for dating. She so wants you."

"I'm not going to dignify that with an answer."

"Presumably though that's Little Miss Yellow Hat from the dating app I set you up with? No need to answer, that was a rhetorical question. You should definitely go over later and get better acquainted. I am a genius."

I smiled, and although I didn't tell him, I was flattered by her attention. It was only about half an hour later when I saw the group she was with gathering their coats. She came back over. "We're off in a min, but perhaps we could have a drink some time?"

"Well why not now?" said Tom. He looked at his watch. "I was just saying to Cameron that I needed to make a move – I need to feed the cat. But she is gasping for another G and T."

Pip smiled in a way that made her look quite cute, and went to the bar. I kicked Tom under the table.

"Your bloody cat!"

"I know, brilliant aren't I?" His eyes sparkled with mischief, and he gathered his possessions. As Pip returned to the table with two drinks, he made his excuses and sped out of the restaurant.

"Won't your friends mind?" I asked her.

"No, they've all got kids, so they're off home to pay the babysitters. It's a bit early for going home for my liking."

"Their loss is my gain I suppose. At least I have a better idea of what to do when we're talking in person."

"Yes," she said thoughtfully, "online dating is an interesting one isn't it? There is something fantastically rational about listing your likes and dislikes and scanning people's profiles. But what about chemistry? I'm not sure you can get a real sense of that through texts and images alone."

"Have you met up with anyone from the app before?" I was genuinely interested to know her experience.

She sighed. "Only one. She seemed quite interesting, a teacher like me. We met for an early lunch one Saturday. Within half an hour she'd downed three pints of Stella and was away with the fairies. Not sure if it was nerves or what, but the last I saw of her was when I poured her into a cab and beat a hasty retreat home."

"Classy."

"How about you? Have you met anyone?"

I smiled. "I have now."

She told me about her job at the local secondary school where she taught English to smelly teenagers, as she described them. It was clear from her tone that she was fond of them though. I told her about my work at the hub. We laughed and ordered more drinks, discussing our own school days and the teachers we inevitably had crushes on.

"I'll never forget that History teacher. I suppose she was only about 25, but she just seemed so sophisticated and intelligent. Her hair was always perfect in a way that suggested that she didn't really work hard to make it that way. She had a gorgeous smile, and always made time for her class members," Pip said, grinning bashfully at the memory.

"For me it wasn't a teacher actually, but the librarian. I guess she must have been in her 30s. She came to work in an old VW Beetle, and wore thick round glasses like John Lennon in a way that made her seem uber cool. Well, at least to me. I'm sure I spent more time than was healthy lurking round the library. That said, I became very well read for a 13-year-old." I was about to continue, when my phone vibrated. It was around 11pm, so I wondered who was contacting me at this time of night. I looked to see Tom's name flash up, expecting some lewd suggestion of what I was up to, but instead I found an urgent looking message.

//Check the news now. It's Sara. Come over now.//

A panicked bead of sweat appeared from nowhere and trickled down my forehead. There was something in the words he'd chosen that told me something bad had happened. I knew it was the night of the vote, but this didn't sound political.

"Sorry, just had an urgent message from a friend. Do you mind if I quickly check something?"

"No," said Pip, "go ahead." The waiters were beginning to put chairs on tables, and candles were being blown out and replaced with the neon strip lighting designed to destroy all atmosphere and get rid of customers asap.

I fumbled with my phone, and brought up the news. When I saw the headline I thought I had slipped into some parallel universe.

MP SARA LORENZO STABBED ON THE STEPS OF THE COMMONS

I tapped the story, hoping for some explanation of what had happened and reassurance that she was ok. I was disappointed to find that there was very little text underneath.

News reports are coming in that the Shadow Health Secretary, Sara Lorenzo, has been stabbed as she left the Commons this evening.

As yet little is known about the attack, which took place just minutes after Lorenzo and her party defeated the Government on their controversial health bill.

This is a developing story and we will publish more details as soon as they become available.

I stood up. Pip looked quizzically at me. "Sorry," I said, trying to remember I should somehow explain my actions, "a friend has been badly hurt. I have to go." Before she could say any more, I grabbed my coat and bag and made for the door. As it closed behind me I thought I heard her ask if there was anything she could do. I fled the scene, relieved that Tom's place was only a few minutes walk away.

As I walked up the stairs to his apartment, Tom was already at the open door, cup of tea in hand. "Come in, darling, sit down."

"Have there been any further updates?"

"No, it seems there has been a lot of confusion. Westminster is completely locked down - there are suggestions this may be part of a terrorist attack."

"Oh God. I need to go to London. Now." I began to stand up.

Tom put a hand on my knee. "Look, stop, sit down. Drink your tea and we'll work out what we're going to do. Whatever happens, you're not going anywhere without me." My eyes filled with tears at his kindness. He turned and put the TV on. The rolling news channel was reporting the facts, such as they were, over and over, along with library footage of Sara outside the Commons.

"Oh God Tom, it's like she's dead. What if she is dead? What if they are keeping it quiet for now while they sort everything out?" My hands were shaking.

"Shh, come on now, love, you know what they're like, it'll be a flesh wound, but they'll be keeping everything under wraps, especially if they are worried about terrorists."

A reporter came into focus, on a nondescript street in London. The man addressed the live link to the studio. He said, "We've been moved away from the Palace of Westminster. The whole area has been evacuated, with access only granted to the emergency services. There is no information being released at all at this point. However, I can tell you that I have personally seen teams of armed Police officers being driven into the exclusion zone, and a little earlier, we saw a helicopter fly in. We are told by a source that it landed briefly, for less than a minute, and then we saw it fly out and away." A grainy VT of a helicopter flying through the dark was shown on the split screen. "We believe this may have been an air ambulance, but we haven't had this clarified yet. No news as yet as to the condition of Sara Lorenzo, who has reportedly been stabbed. Back to you in the studio."

The anchor in the studio was joined by a man she introduced as a security expert. Tom muted the endless speculation because, for now, that's all it was.

"They're not going to say where they're taking her are they?" I said, more as a statement than a question. Tom shook his head.

"No. But I reckon they'll get her away from Westminster if they can and out of the limelight."

"What if we went to London and just started checking the hospitals?"

"It's no use, Cam. Look." He pointed at the TV where the ticker tape along the bottom reported that all trains and public transport in and out of London had been severely affected by the situation with extra security. Images flashed up of gridlocked roads, blue flashing lights and drops of rain distorting the view through the news camera. "Even if we managed to get as far as London by car, we still don't know which hospital she'll be in, and they wouldn't let us near her."

"What can we do?" I put my head in my hands and focused on the space between my feet. The world shrank into a square of beige carpet. Tom shuffled up next to me and put his arm around me. I don't know how long we sat like that for. The hours passed with us glued to the news updates. Slowly, small details began to come through in the reports. Grainy shots, which must have been filmed with a very long lens, showed a blue tent with calm activity outside. This was the place it had happened. She had stood just there only a few hours before when someone, male or female, we didn't know, had chosen, made an active decision to attack her. Her body pierced in a mindless act of violence. I couldn't help but imagine the scene, the devastation, the pain, the fear. I wondered if she had cried out, screamed, fought back. Maybe she wordlessly sank to the floor as her assailant ran. News reports suggested that the attacker was yet to be identified or caught, so armed teams could be seen in all shots of a rain streaked London on the TV screen.

"Do you still have her number?" Tom asked me gently.

"Yes, of course. But it's been too long."

"Has it? I'm not sure any of that matters now darling."

"She'll have people around her, her new, um, girlfriend or whatever." My mind drifted to the publicity images of that radio journalist.

"Just let her know you're thinking of her." He got up and walked into the kitchen, putting the kettle on for the umpteenth time. I picked up my phone and stared at it. After all that had happened, would a call make any difference at all? At that moment it vibrated into life, making me jump.

//Cam, just seen the news. You ok? H xx//

Hayley. She was the last person I was expecting to hear from. It had been weeks since that last day in Ibiza, and I'd not heard from her since then, nor expected to. I picked the phone up and rang the number that had been neglected for so long. I didn't expect an answer. It went straight through to answer phone. I stifled the thought that perhaps the person I was calling would never listen to this message. "It's Cam. I've seen the news. Of course, I've seen the news. Are you ok? Stupid, sorry, you're obviously not ok. God I don't even know what to say. Just I want you to be ok, I'm sending you all the love I have. You don't have to call me if you don't want to but it would be just so good to hear your voice. You know where I am." I ended the call and clutched the phone to me.

I looked over to Tom who was checking his own phone for messages. He came back with a cup of tea for each of us. "You should try and get some sleep really." I didn't answer, we both knew the likelihood of that. His phone beeped again.

I looked at the ever present clock in the corner of the news coverage. It was past 2am, minutes ticking ever onward with no real news to speak of. "Who's texting you at this time of night?"

Tom quickly put his phone in his pocket. "Oh, you know, no one. Hey, look, put the sound back on."

I scrambled for the remote control, and turned up the volume. A flustered looking reporter appeared on the screen. ".... and we are now hearing that the individual who attacked MP Sara Lorenzo has been apprehended by police, and early indications are that he was acting alone and this is not part of a co-ordinated attack on the Commons. Armed police will continue to stand guard overnight as a precaution, but the exclusion zone around the Palace of Westminster is being slowly opened up."

Shots were shown of people milling around in the night time streets. Some had been unable to get anywhere because of restrictions on the Tube and bus systems.

"Well, that's good news at least," said Tom quietly.

"Not so sure it's good. But perhaps less bad I suppose. Still nothing on her though. I just need to know if she's..." I couldn't say the word.

"As soon as they have any firm information they'll share it, Cam. I know this is cold comfort, but the saying that bad news travels fast is there for a reason." His phone beeped again and he checked it. He caught his breath and then paused for a moment. He looked at me. "She's in St Mark's in greater London."

I stood and put on my coat. "We'll take my car," he said, "you're in no fit state to drive."

"Thank you."

Chapter 25

We'd been on the road for 25 minutes before either of us spoke again. "How do you know where she is? They're still not reporting anything about her or her whereabouts on the news."

He indicated and pulled into the outside lane of the motorway. "You probably don't want to know." He adjusted the volume of the radio station. "Someone owes me a favour, and I called it in."

"You have fingers in so many pies, Tom." I felt lighter to finally be doing something. Watching the white lines dash beneath the cars became almost meditative. The words of the announcer coming from the high quality speakers merged together into a low hum. There were other cars on the road, but many stretches were empty. I felt my eyes begin to close, safe in the knowledge that even if I drifted off, I was still moving closer to Sara. How she felt about me for now simply didn't matter. I needed to see her and tell her how I felt.

"Cam, sweetie, wake up." I felt a gentle hand on my shoulder. I brought my hand to my mouth, paranoid that my awkward sleeping position had given way to drool. I opened my eyes. We were parked outside a service station, where bright lights invited us into the warm soulless depths. "I need a coffee, and to check the best route. Sorry to stop and disturb you. Hope you don't mind."

I shook my head, still not quite awake.

"You look like you could do with something hot and sweet," said Tom. I nodded. We sat at a Formica table. He consulted his phone, while I sipped sweet tea and ate a currant bun. I hadn't eaten in hours. He didn't take his eyes from his phone as he spoke to me. "I think the best thing to do is dump the car here, at Cockfosters. We can get the tube in from there – the congestion has eased. It's our best hope of getting there with minimum stress." He had transitioned into work mode. I could see why he was such a good researcher. I remember him once telling me he had been courted by MI5. I laughed. But it came back to me now. Perhaps it wasn't so unlikely after all.

It wasn't long before we were being sucked into the belly of the city through its intestinal tunnels. The tube was awash with people trying to get home, having been stuck in various parts of the city during the incident. People looked weary but somehow bright-eyed. The adrenalin coursing through everyone was palpable. We emerged onto a street, lit yellow with the lights working unaffected by the drama of the evening. I checked my phone now I had signal once more and jumped to see a new headline.

//MP Sara Lorenzo reported as in a critical but stable condition following stabbing//

I gasped, and thrust my phone towards Tom's face. "Good," he said, "she's alive. Thank God. Now let's get you to her." My legs gave way slightly, and I thought for a moment I might just sink to the floor in relief. But it was short-lived. Critical was not a good word. What did that really mean? Tom glanced at me, grabbed my arm, and we marched with purpose towards the hospital's bright frontage. In front of the main entrance was a host of photographers and reporters, keen to get the news as it happened. We had just missed a short press statement which had been given by one of Westminster's media team on the steps of the hospital. Journalists were scattered along the steps shouting into phones, speaking into cameras and writing notes.

"Cam," said Tom, "put your hood up and hold my hand."

"What?"

"Just do it. You don't want them to recognise you do you?" I thought of the grainy pictures they will all have seen and no doubt committed to memory. I hurriedly lifted the hood to my head, and he grabbed my hand and tugged me swiftly through the crowd into the foyer. There were a substantial number of security officers present, as well as two armed police officers who were trying not to look too threatening to the handful of visitors coming in and out, and the dark-eyed patients with drips hurrying to the doorstep so they could have a cigarette. Tom started rambling on about visiting Uncle Terry, and directing us to the coronary ward. I looked at him and then away. He gave me his best 'I know what I'm doing' look so I just nodded and smiled and followed him. Still gripping my hand he pulled me into a lift.

As the doors closed I dropped my hood. "So what are we going to do when we get to the coronary ward?" I asked.

He smiled. "Did you notice what else shares a floor with the coronary unit?" He let go of my hand, and pointed to the panel next to the lift controls. Floor seven was labelled as hosting the coronary unit and the trauma unit. If there had been a penny, it had now dropped. Of course, that is where she would have been taken after this kind of injury.

"God bless Uncle Terry." I said under my breath.

Somewhere inside I wondered about what had happened that night with Caroline. It felt hazy now in the sharp white blaze of the hospital lift. I never even got the chance to see her in hospital. I felt my jaw clench, trying to halt the horrors of what I would find on the others side of the lift doors. When the doors opened we found ourselves in a clinical space. We couldn't see anyone, but there was a gentle hum of activity present. Footsteps, machinery, murmurs.

We were into uncharted territory. "Come on," said Tom. He pulled me towards the trauma department, and I wondered if he had a plan for getting through the inevitable security barrier. He walked with purpose to the nurses' station.

"I'm here to see Sara Lorenzo," he stated. A nurse looked up at him, her face emotionless.

"Just bear with me for a moment." She disappeared behind some swinging doors. Tom and I took deep breaths at the same time. I looked down and found my hands clasped together so tightly that my knuckles were white. She returned a few minutes later. "Can I ask who you are?"

I looked up at Tom, and then realised that it would need to be me who did this bit. "Well, I'm Sara's, er, friend. I'm Cam. I mean, I'm Cameron Strawbank. If she's well enough to see me, I'd really like to see her. If she wants to see me. Obviously if she's not up to it, then fine. I just wanted her to know I'm here." I felt Tom tug my sleeve. I stopped speaking.

The nurse paused and gave me a hard stare, before vanishing again through the swinging doors. She returned within a few minutes.

"You have 10 minutes, and that's it. Come this way." Tom hung back, and, wide eyed, I followed the nurse through a maze of corridors and through various sets of doors. We must have passed police and security, but I was just focusing on what I was about to be presented. I had no idea what I was about to see, how she would be, whether she was even conscious. The nurse knocked on a pale blue door with a window in it. A man with messy curly hair and a slightly greying beard opened the door.

"Cameron?" I nodded. The nurse retreated. "It's good to see you." He put his hands into the pockets of his jeans. "Sorry, of course, you don't know who I am. I'm Matthew."

"Matthew? Her, um,"

"Yes, her ex-husband. I hadn't realised I was still down as her next-of-kin. But then, I guess, who else would be?" He paused. I could see the end of the bed behind him, but nothing more. "Are you ok? You look a bit pale."

"So do you," I said. He smiled and rubbed his eyes.

"Yes, it's been a crazy few hours. Come on through. She's not long out of surgery, so she's only partially aware of what's going on."

Sara looked small in the hospital bed. She was surrounded by medical technology and a dizzying array of bleeps and lights and monitors. Her face had a yellow hue, although there were still traces of her trademark lipstick there. Her eyes were half open. I wasn't sure if she was looking at me or not. The heart monitor reassured me as I walked towards her and sat down in the warm chair that must have been Matthew's until I arrived. I picked up her hand, and her head turned towards me. She made a noise, but nothing that made any sense.

"Shh Sara love, don't try and speak," said Matthew. "Cameron's here to see you. She's just going to stay for a few minutes."

I sat motionless for a moment, wondering what to do and what to say. I took a breath. "Sara, I'm so sorry. What a day. As soon as I found out where you were, I came. I just wanted you to know that you're not alone. I care about you. You know that." I turned her hand over and stroked her palm gently. I watched her eyes slowly close.

"Thanks for coming, Cam. She'll appreciate it."

"Will she remember?"

"That doesn't matter. I know we haven't met before. But I know what you mean to her." He pushed his hair off his glistening forehead. "You look surprised."

"I am. I wasn't sure she'd want to see me."

"You've got to know, she's been miserable since you two broke up. I know it's been a mess. I know you've both been hurt. But that doesn't negate how you feel now. Sorry, I know, it's odd me saying all this when you don't know me."

"So, how is she?"

"She's actually in a pretty good state considering what happened." He went on to explain that after she was brought to the hospital she went into theatre where surgeons repaired the wound and some internal bleeding. The operation had lasted several hours and she had received a blood transfusion to replace what she'd lost in the attack.

"God, it's just, I don't know, just shocking." Matthew walked over and put his hand on my shoulder.

"I heard on the news they got the guy who did it," he said.

The ever efficient nurse appeared at the door. "It's time for me to go," I said. "Thank you for letting me see her." I leaned down and gently kissed Sara's cheek. Somewhere beneath the disinfectant hospital smell, I could smell the real Sara. "I'll see you soon," I whispered.

"Here, give me your number. I'll let you know how she's doing."

I found Tom sitting on a plastic chair busily texting. He looked up. "Come on, Cam, I've got us a hotel."

Chapter 26

I woke with a sore head and a dry mouth. I was alone in the twin room Tom had managed to find. I checked my phone to see a message from him telling me that he was already having breakfast. After a quick shower, I threw on the clothes I'd worn the day before, and headed down to join him.

"The coffee had better be good," I said, as I sat down.

Tom smiled. "I've had worse."

It was good to sit and eat without the gnawing anxiety I'd experienced the night before. "I know she's not out of the woods yet, but I feel more hopeful this morning. Lighter."

"Good. I'm glad. Listen, I'm going to need to go back and get to work. It's up to you – if you want to go and see Sara again this morning, you can get the train back. Or you can come back with me after breakfast."

"I'll stay. I want to see her again. Hopefully I'll be able to be with her a bit longer today."

"Sorry I can't come with you this time."

"No, don't be sorry, Tom, you've done so much. You have no idea how much I appreciate it. I'll be fine on the train." I glanced down and noticed Tom had been reading the papers. The front pages were dominated by news of Sara's stabbing. "It was him wasn't it?"

"Sorry?"

"It was that journalist who told you what hospital she was at wasn't it?"

Tom sighed. "Yes. He owed me."

"Have you seen him?"

"No, definitely not. Never again. I knew that you wouldn't be able to rest until you'd seen her, and I guessed he'd be the kind of person who'd have the info we needed. I asked, and he answered." Tom put aside the plate he had cleared. "Don't forget to put your hood up again when you go into the hospital. And be quick." I took another mouthful of toast. "Are you angry that I contacted him?"

I chewed and swallowed before I spoke. "No. I suppose I had just hoped I would never come across him again. I tried to remove him from my memory. What he did." I dipped my knife into the apricot jam. "But now, he's done something good. It feels weird."

"Don't over-think it," said Tom. "It doesn't pay to do that."

"Ha," I laughed, "I think over-thinking may be my strong suit."

I waved Tom goodbye, and an hour later I was back in Sara's hospital room. She was alone this time. Her eyes were open. I smiled, and sat beside her. "You look better."

"Were you here before?" She asked in a whisper. I nodded. "I thought I dreamt you."

"I was here. I think you were somewhere in a cloud of opiates. It's so good to hear your voice. I was afraid."

"Me too," she said. "They say I've been lucky."

"I guess it depends on how you look at it, Sara. It could have been so much worse." She closed her eyes. Her hand was still in mine, and soon I heard her breathing become deep and regular. It was going to be a while before she was enjoying a glass of wine in a swanky London bar again.

I leaned over and laid my head beside hers. I spoke softly into the pillow that was strewn with her hair. "I know you can't hear me. I miss you." With my eyes closed I could pretend we were somewhere else. "I love you."

Getting on the train back to London that afternoon was so hard. I wanted to stay, but I had to get back to the hub, to my flat, to my responsibilities. Like pulling a plaster off a reluctant wound, I chose a fast train, and was back in less than two hours. The next day's papers were full of stories about Sara's swift recovery, surrounded by family and friends. I wasn't sure if I fitted into either of those categories.

The days that followed passed in a blur of my day job, food, sleep and calls with Matthew. We spoke most evenings. It was simple information – she managed to eat a proper meal one day, she got out of bed the next. Eventually she was well enough to speak to me herself. It was an oddly polite conversation. Matthew was at the other end with her, and I was at work. She told me her views on the food – not favourable – and I told her about the hub and the forthcoming launch event we were planning to get a bit of publicity, and hopefully raise some funds.

Chapter 27

"Oh you look so much better," I said, seeing her sitting up in bed.

"Well, it has been almost a week, Cam. Thanks for coming," said Sara in a voice that made her sound much more like her normal self.

"Wow, loving the robe. Where on earth is that from?"

"Ah this old thing... Well, if I'm honest, I was fed up with those awful hospital gowns and the smell of disinfectant. I gave Matthew my credit card, and told him to buy my usual perfume and an outrageously extravagant dressing gown. You like it?"

"I love it, you look like a 1930s film star in a lavish convalescence home."

"Now, that I will take as a compliment, Cameron darling."

"All you need now is an expensive cigarette in a long black holder."

"Oh God don't. I haven't had one of those since I was a teenager. Ugh. Foul." She shook her head at the thought. My mind escaped momentarily into a cloud of smoke curling away from Hayley's mouth. Guilt.

"I never even tried one."

"Bless you, Cam, you're such an innocent. See that jug over there? Any chance you can go and fill it with water? I have to drink so much at the moment with all the painkillers."

I returned a few moments later with a plastic jug full of tepid water.

"Sorry, Sara, they don't do ice on the NHS."

She sighed. "Roll on discharge. You know, they say I can go home in a day or two if my blood tests come back clear."

"Oh that would be wonderful, it really would. But how will you cope at home on your own?"

"I'll cross that bridge when I come to it. Matthew has threatened to move in. I mean, can you imagine?"

"He loves you."

"Of course. And I him. But our days of living together are over. He has his own family to look after. No, I'll work something out." She waved her hand as if dismissing me. A door slammed.

"You know, I could always..."

"No, Cam, no. I'll be fine."

There was a pause. Neither of us spoke, and then Sara appeared to wilt. "Come on, back into bed. You need to rest."

"What are you doing?"

"I'm fluffing up the pillows like they do on telly in hospital."

"Excellent, healthcare a la Holby. I like it. I think perhaps I do need to sleep."

"It's ok," I said, "there's a nice looking café opposite the hospital that I've been meaning to try out. I'll buy a paper and have a cup of tea. Sleep well." I stroked her hair from her forehead and then left, closing her door gently.

Unrelenting London traffic juddered past the front window of the café. I set the paper down in front of me, but couldn't focus on reading it. She didn't even let me complete my offer to help her. I wasn't even sure what I was going to offer. But whatever I had, she didn't want it. I pulled out my phone and called Tom. "Hey, Cam, you ok? How's London?"

"Yeah, just having a cuppa while she sleeps." I was mindful not to mention her name out loud in a public place.

"How is she?"

"Oh so much better. You should see her today, she looks like a star of the silver screen. I think perhaps we should see if they'll put a chaise longue in her room."

"Ha, sounds like she's getting back to her old self. Are you ok?"

"Yep."

"Oh dear."

"What? I'm fine." I shuffled round the sugar sachets on the table in front of me while Tom waited. "How do you always know?"

"I can tell by the tone of your voice."

"It's just that I don't know who I am to her. We talk and she lets me in to a certain point and then somewhere a door shuts. It's like she's keeping me at arm's length."

"She's still recovering. Perhaps you're being a bit over-sensitive?" His voice was gentle.

"I know. But today, honestly, it's not that. This is about how she feels about me. I don't know, I just thought perhaps, with everything that had happened, that we might be able to start again. What happened to her seemed to make all that went before mean less." I stirred my tea for the fourth time. "But she feels differently. I've been friend zoned."

"Oh hun, you can't make any assumptions. Just think about what has happened in the last week. All the medical treatment, all the press attention. And remember, just because the story about you and her has blown over, who's to say it wouldn't whip up again if you were seen together in public? Have you considered that she might be protecting you?"

"Yeah, I guess."

"You sound like a teenager," he said with a tut. I laughed. "Look, I've got to go to a meeting, but hang on, Cam. You'll be ok. Have a Danish pastry."

"Thanks, Tom. I will. See you."

Chapter 28

The days passed slowly and uneventfully, my focus on the launch event for the community hub. The day itself was eagerly anticipated by all involved. As the morning of the event dawned, the sun shone. It was a new beginning for so many people, and hopefully for me too. I arrived at the hub early and unlocked the doors. Soon there would be a hubbub of activity, with the caterers due to arrive and the rest of the volunteers. I allowed myself to look around the empty room, which looked so unlikely as the source of the hope me and the team wanted to create. But create it we would. The sound system had already been installed – we wanted this to feel like a party for the community – so once I had made myself a cup of tea, I started the music. It filled the draughty room with energy and helped me focus on the job in hand.

Within a few hours, the hall was seething with people. There were delicious smells coming from the kitchen, where a community bakery had set up shop for the day. There was a careers advice stall, a benefits support stand, a voluntary library and one of the health visitors from the local clinic. An instructor who ran a business nearby was setting up, offering Tai Chi classes to those who came along, as part of an ongoing offer to help people enhance mindfulness and fitness in a non-threatening way. Simon was smiling and hanging out bunting that looked like it had probably been used for at least 30 years.

He walked over to where I stood. "What do you think, Cam?" he asked?

"Do you know what, Simon, I think it looks great! I can't believe we've come this far. After all that work, and our ambitious plans. It would seem that optimism really does pay off after all."

He smiled. "Yes," he said, "I think it does. Thanks for all you've done, Cam. We really wouldn't have come this far without you." Before I could respond, one of the volunteers approached us and asked if she could open the doors to the public.

"Yes please," I said, "let them in." And in they came. Lots of familiar faces flowed through the doors, eyeing each of the stands and making a beeline to the kitchen hatch. A variety of sweet and savoury goodies were now on display and children were enthusiastically dragging their parents over for a closer look.

A face that I had come to know well approached me. She was the woman who had been so shy that first time I volunteered at the food bank. "Cameron, thank you, this is amazing," she said, her eyes shining.

"Oh really, Fatema, I'm just so pleased to see you here. And look at your little ones, how they've grown."

"Yes," she said, proudly looking down at them. "I have news." She gave me a broad smile.

"Really?" I asked.

"Yes. I just heard yesterday. I got a job as a teaching assistant at their school three days a week." I could see the pride in her face.

"Wow, Fatema, that's fantastic, well done."

"Thank you. It's so good to know I can better support my family. And I wanted to thank you, for believing I could do it." Her face flushed as she spoke to me.

"But really, you know, it was all you."

"But you and Simon and the others gave me the confidence. I had stopped applying for jobs, I just didn't think I was good enough." She swallowed back tears. "So here I am. Thank you."

"Well, you're welcome. If ever you want to do some volunteering here to help others, then you'd be really welcome."

"I will." She beamed, and let her children drag her over to where some gingerbread men were being given out.

I couldn't help but smile. "Looks like today is going well," came a voice from behind me. I looked round.

"Hayley," I said, blood rushing to my face, "what are you doing here?"

"I came to see what all the fuss was about. Looks like you've done an amazing job." She grinned.

"Thank you." I paused. "I'm sorry I never texted you back."

"Oh, don't worry, you had far too much on your plate to worry about me. I just wanted you to know you weren't alone. I figured that no response meant you had someone."

I nodded. "Yes, Tom. He was great actually."

"Good. How is she?"

"Ok I think. It's been a while since I've seen her." I dropped my head as I spoke.

"Oh, so you didn't?" She let the sentence hang.

"Her recovery will take a long time. It's hard for her to travel."

"Yes, I suppose it must be."

"What about you?" I asked, looking around for Max. I didn't know what he looked like, but couldn't identify anyone nearby.

"I'm fine thanks. Taking some time for myself."

"You mean alone?"

She nodded. "I told him no. You were right. I was running away."

"We both were."

"Yes," she said. "But no tearful reunion?"

"No," I said, "it's too late."

"Who for?" she asked.

"Cam, can I grab you?" Simon's voice cut through the moment. "The press are here and it would be great if you could give a short statement. Do you have a minute?"

"Sure." I turned back to Hayley. "I'll be right back." She nodded.

20 minutes later I had finished with the keen young journalist. It was something of a new experience after having been a prisoner in my own home because of paparazzi not so long before. I looked around the room, but couldn't see Hayley. I spent a few minutes double checking I hadn't missed her, but she was nowhere to be found. It seemed strange. I replayed the conversation in my head. She'd asked about a tearful reunion, and she meant with Sara. Didn't she? I heard my phone chime, a text message notification.

//Sorry babe, had to run, got a date. Glad to see you doing well. H xx//

Chapter 29

"This is the midday news on Radio Four. The Prime Minister has called a General Election."

I switched off the radio on the shelf in my office and picked up my phone. Sara picked up within one ring. "Did you hear the news?"

"That's why I was ringing you," I said, "what took him so long?"

"Maybe he thinks now's his chance for a second term. Who knows, Cam, but one thing is for sure, it's going to be a manic few months."

"Did you have any idea it would be now?"

"No. I mean, the strategists have been planning for various scenarios, but specifically an election now? No, I didn't expect that. Perhaps he's trying to harness some of the support for MPs that has been generated since, well, you know."

"Mmm, would be a bit cynical though wouldn't it?"

"I guess. But you know better than most that anything is fair game when it comes to politics. I'm just glad I have a reasonable majority. I'm not going to be able to commit the same level of time and energy to campaigning as I normally do, more's the pity."

I could hear the regret in her voice. There had been times in the past few weeks when I had thought that she might consider leaving politics after what had happened. But, apart from one late night conversation, her resolve hadn't weakened. There was something impressive about it. I wasn't sure I would have done the same.

"How are you getting on at home now?"

"Better thanks. I even managed to make myself beans on toast the other day, which is a real achievement."

"That sounds terribly mundane for you, Sara."

"If it helps, I garnished it with some parsley."

"God," I laughed, "don't let the papers know that."

"Noted Strawbank. Perhaps it's time I had a proper meal. I'm improving every day now, and it would be wonderful to do my hair, put make-up on and go out. You could come with me?"

"Where? Not London, we might be seen."

"Oh let them see us. Just friends having dinner. Nothing wrong with that."

"Well, yes, I guess so." I chewed my lip. Just friends. I dropped my head to my free hand.

"Anyway, I was thinking Mallington would be easier anyway, since I'm here at the moment. There's an Italian place just opened up, and I'd like to give it a try. You up for it?"

"Yeah. Sure."

"You could sound a bit keener, Cam. I can always try it out alone." I heard her chuckle in the background.

"Sorry, just a bit busy and tired. Of course I'd like to."

"Great. So, this Saturday?"

"Fine with me."

"Lovely, now I'd better go, my agent is calling on my other line. See you Saturday, Cam."

The call ended. I chewed my lip. I sighed, and then noted the date in my diary. As if I would forget it. Over the inevitable cup of tea that followed, I thought back over the past few months. It hadn't ended as I'd planned.

Chapter 30

My feet were heavy walking towards the Italian restaurant. She arrived just as I did.

"Wow," I said before I could stop myself, "you look amazing. So much better than last time I saw you." It had been a few weeks, and the elegant, well-dressed and presented woman in front of me with colour in her cheeks looked like a different person.

Sara smiled. "Well, I thought the least I deserved was some new clothes and a hairdo. Come here. You're not normally so reluctant to have a hug."

"Sorry, it's just so, strange, I suppose, after everything. You know." I spoke these words into her hair as I put my arms around her, taking in her scent, which was thankfully unchanged. I allowed my eyes to close momentarily.

We chatted politely over our starters, which were without reproach. There was something impersonal about our discussion of politics and how my work was going. Like friends who hadn't seen each other in a while.

"I don't know about you," said Sara, her eyes sparkling, "but I think we deserve something a bit celebratory."

"Well, why the hell not, you deserve to celebrate. And can I say, you look triumphant." Sara laughed and called over a waiter to order some expensive champagne.

"Triumphant?" She furrowed her brow. "How utterly un-alluring."

"Perhaps I chose the wrong word. But then, I suppose I'm no longer the person you want to be alluring anyway."

We both took a sip from our champagne glasses. I felt my cheeks flush.

"Really? Is there someone else you're applying your charms to?" she said, raising an eyebrow.

"God no. But I know I burnt my bridges with you. I know that. It was all just too much wasn't it?"

Our main courses arrived, so there was a stay of execution before Sara replied. As the waiter left she closed her eyes slowly, and then opened them.

"Yes. It was." she said. "Far too much. And you weren't the only one who burnt bridges. I thought that staying away from you would be the right thing to do. But now I look back on it all, and I should have come to you and ignored those wretched party suits. What do they know of real life? They live among the shadows and have a private life. Why shouldn't I have one too?"

"Good for you. But I can see why you did what you did."

"And perhaps, after a while, I began to see why you did what you did," she said. She looked at me, her eyes sad. I looked down at my plate. It was a vision of edible perfection, but I couldn't bring myself to start eating.

"It's funny isn't it. All these months later and things seem so different." I looked up and smiled back at her serious face.

"I began to think, when I was in hospital, that perhaps it wasn't too late. You came for me, you spent time with me, and showed how much you cared. I didn't know what was going on for a while, the drugs really sent me into some strange imaginings."

"Yes, I remember how dilated your pupils were, especially early on. It was like you were lost," I said, remembering.

"Perhaps I was." Sara looked down at her plate, and began to eat. I made a show of cutting a piece off the steak in front of me, but I couldn't really bring myself to put it in my mouth. "But you know, towards the end of my stay, I realised it really was too late. We had both lost too much to go back."

"I see," I said. I put down my fork again, and opted for more champagne. It was really the only thing I could think of to do. It would have to be a liquid lunch. I would have to think of an excuse for hardly eating a thing.

"It's been hard these last few weeks, beginning to put everything back together again. I've started doing some work again, attending debates and votes, running constituency surgeries. It's been good. But there has been something missing. I thought maybe it was confidence."

"Well, it would be understandable under the circumstances. I do hope you're not overdoing it. You were so unwell," I said in a stiff voice.

"God you sound like my mother, bless her dear departed soul. No, I'm not. And there's nothing wrong with my confidence."

"Oh?"

"No." She was about to go on, but somewhere amongst the champagne and the anxiety and lack of food, my head began to swim.

"Sorry, just give me a minute." I stood abruptly, my carefully placed napkin falling to the floor, and walked as fast as my wobbly legs could take me out of the restaurant and into the cold air. I leaned against the outer wall of the restaurant and took a couple of deep breaths. I looked to the sky and asked myself why I was even there. I was contemplating running away, like a scorned teenager, when I heard a voice beside me.

"Cam? Are you ok? Sorry, it took me a few moments to get to you – I've still not got the speed to sprint quite at that speed after the surgery."

"Look," I said, unable to look at the woman to my side, "I am happy to hear you are working stuff out, and it's good to know that you think that we may have had a chance if things had worked out differently. But the thing is, they didn't. Everything fell apart for me, Sara, everything. I've had to put everything back together. And I've done a good job." I could feel tears beginning, but I carried on. Now I had started I couldn't stop. "I have told myself time and again that it is too late and that I have moved on. And I had started to begin to think that it was really true. But these last few weeks, I can't help it, it has just become blindingly obvious that I am not over you. I love you. And I know it's too late. But I can't sit here and listen to you talk about how complete your life is. How sorted you are. I'm sorry. I have to go."

"Stop." She placed a hand on my arm as I made to move away. "Ok, look, listen, let me just tell you one thing, and then you can go if you want to." I kept staring ahead. She took my silence as permission to go on. "What I wanted to say was that I wasn't missing my confidence, I wasn't missing anything about myself. I have been phenomenally lucky to survive what happened. My life is now almost exactly the same as it was. The problem with that is that I have changed. And I miss you. I've come to realise that really, in life, telling ourselves it's too late is an excuse for inaction. It's never really too late." Her hand moved down my forearm to my fingers and she grasped them in her own. I focused my attention on my shoes, trying to make sense of what she was saying. "So you see, what I want to tell you is that I do love you, and I want you in my life, and I think we can do this."

There was a beat.

"Cam, please, look at me." I slowly brought my tear stained face to meet hers. She placed her hand on my cheek and stroked a tear away gently. "Please, can I kiss you?"

"You're asking? That's a first," I said. I gave her a half smile.

"Well, as I said, I have changed a bit. For the better perhaps." Her eyebrows rose. "Is that a yes?"

"Yes." I looked at her properly for the first time since I had left the restaurant. "Please."

Our lips came together in one fluid movement, and I felt for a moment that I would weep all over again when she put her arms around me and held me close. It was a few moments before we broke contact.

"But what about the party? The newspapers? We can't do this in secret can we?"

"Sod the party. Look, I've made that mistake once and I'm not doing it again. People will either vote for me or not, but I know now that really what I want is you. If you'll have me."

"You bloody idiot, of course I will," I said. "When was the last time someone literally swooned in front of you in a restaurant?" She threw her head back and laughed that glorious unrestrained joyful laugh of hers. When she stopped she gave me a searing kiss that meant only one thing, and that sure as hell was that we weren't going to be finishing our meal.

"Come on, Cam, I need you." She grabbed my hand roughly and tugged me in the direction of her house. We both giggled, practically skipping over the cobblestones, gently in her case. Once in her house we moved swiftly to the bedroom.

I peeled her clothes slowly from her, stroking her softly, fearful of hurting her. The scar was immediately evident. Red, angry, raised. It zigzagged across her midriff. She caught me looking.

"It will fade in time I'm told." she said.

"You know," I said, as we both looked at it, "I think it makes you even more beautiful." I gently kissed her abdomen and the area around the scar that had nearly taken her from me forever.

"Oh?" She questioned.

"It's a sign of your strength, your survival, your bloody-mindedness."

"Oh Cam, I've missed you. I'm so sorry."

"No more sorries," I said, "it's all done with. It's just us now." She smiled and nodded at me.

I peppered kisses down her thighs, enjoying the guttural sounds coming from deep within her when I drew my tongue into her most sensitive place. She trembled in a way I hadn't witnessed before, and she quickly came to a noisy, unruly orgasm.

I moved my head up, to kiss her neck and cheek while she recovered.

"You see," she whispered after a few moments. "It's not too late." I moved up the bed and buried my head in her neck.

"We got here eventually," I said, smiling into her hair, content.

Acknowledgements

A number of people have contributed to the writing, design and publication of this book. Thanks must go to Rosie Collin, whose cover design is beyond my highest hopes. Also to Corinne Yaqub who did the all essential copy editing and proofing. Thank you for your handwritten notes, all the way from sunny Brighton. To Liz Bell who has provided much needed encouragement and inspiration with promotion, thanks for the tiramisu. Thanks to Rebecca Williams who has provided cyber-support of the most helpful kind. And of course, thanks to Clare Lydon for her warm words of encouragement.

Ultimately, none of this would have happened without my wife Rachel and daughter Gwyneth, who keep me focused on what is most important in life. Love. And the people who taught me about love in the first place, my parents and my sister, who have always embraced my creativity.

Find out more at:

www.sallyxerribrooks.wordpress.com

Follow me on Twitter:

@salxerribrooks

Follow me on Instagram:

@mamabearsxb

Like me on Facebook:

www.facebook.com/sallyxerribrooks

Printed in Great Britain
by Amazon